Praise for Sandra Ireland

BONE DEEP

'In themes that ripple through the ages, *Bone Deep* is a taut, contemporary psychological thriller about love, betrayal, female sibling rivalry and bone-grinding, blood-curdling murder' *Sunday Post*

'Gripping from the outset, an atmospheric, fluent book which kept me reading into the small hours'
Dundee Courier, Scottish Book of the Week

'The final chapters take *Bone Deep* from being a beautifully written and thoughtful constructed psychological study into sheer gothic novel nightmare territory . . . a tremendous example of writing and plotting'
Scotland on Sunday

'A psychological thriller drenched in suspense' *Sunday Herald*

'Atmospheric, with a delicious build-up of tension, and beautifully observed throughout' Michael J. Malone, author of *House of Spines*

'Captivating, compelling and infused with Sandra Ireland's evocative sense of place' Noelle Harrison, author of *The Gravity of Love*

BENEATH THE SKIN

'Ireland writes about powerful and troubling subjects and shows how the past can have devastating consequences' *Daily Mail*

'This debut novel is an exceptional calling card . . . an in-depth psychological thriller packed with suspense and loaded with eerie excitement' *Dundee Courier*

'A powerful exploration of PTSD from an astonishing new voice in fiction' Blackwell's Bookshops

A NOTE ON THE AUTHOR

Sandra Ireland was born in Yorkshire, lived for many years in Limerick, and is now based in Carnoustie. She began her writing career as a correspondent on a local newspaper but quickly realised that fiction is much more intriguing than fact. In 2013 Sandra was awarded a Carnegie-Cameron scholarship to study for an MLitt in Writing Practice and Study at the University of Dundee; she graduated with a distinction in 2014. Her work has appeared in various publications such as *New Writing Dundee* and *Furies*, an anthology of women's poetry. She is the author of *Beneath the Skin* (2016) and *Bone Deep* (2018). *The Unmaking of Ellie Rook* is her third novel.

The Unmaking of Ellie Rook

Sandra Ireland

Polygon

First published in Great Britain in 2019 by Polygon,
an imprint of Birlinn Ltd.

West Newington House
10 Newington Road
Edinburgh
EH9 1QS

www.polygonbooks.co.uk

1

ISBN 978 1 84697 482 3
eBook ISBN 978 1 78885 187 9

British Library Cataloguing in Publication Data
A catalogue record for this book is available on request
from the British Library.

Typeset by 3btype.com
Printed and bound by ScandBook AB, Sweden

To my boys, Jamie and Calum.
Love you lots xx

Prologue

June, 2001

'Tell me again, about Finella.'

'I've told you a million times!' my mother laughs, teasing me. We're swinging hands in the dim, cool green of the woods. It's a safe place for stories and secrets: the wind and the screaming gulls can't snatch them away. 'Once upon a time . . .'

'No! I'm too old for once upon a time!'

She squeezes my hand and grins. She has a little gap between her front two teeth that makes her look like a pirate. 'Oh, I forgot, baby – you've a birthday coming up. Eight – so old. I can tell you the gory bits now!'

I'm not sure I want the gory bits, but I don't say that. We perch on a mossy log and listen to the water tumbling over the rocks.

'Imagine this place teeming with deer and game, and wild geese overhead, and the rivers filled with salmon. A rich place, full of rich men. It was the time of Kenneth, King of the Scots, and all his court, and the east coast sea lords. Finella was the daughter of one, wife to another. History remembers the men, but not always the women.'

'And Finella was so strong and wise you named me after her.'

'Yes!' A swift hug. 'You are the one and only Finella Rook! Although Ellie is less of a mouthful for a little girl.'

I scowl at the 'little', but she is already plunging on, and I let myself curl up in the rise and fall of her voice.

'There was another man too, remember. Crathilinth.'

'Finella's son.'

'Yes, executed by King Kenneth for who knows what. Kenneth seriously underestimated Finella's love for her son. Mothers are fierce, and Finella was a huntress. She came up with a cunning plan – we'll call it Plan A. She invited the king to her castle.'

'Tell me that bit again – about the castle.'

'The castle is long gone now, just a pile of stones on a hilltop, not far from here. Grandma Rook told it to me this way: Finella invited the king to a hidden chamber within the castle, a treasure trove of sculptures and curious objects. No doubt he was a bit put out that one of his subjects might have something that he didn't, and the lady possessed the most amazing statue of a little boy, which fired arrows into the air when you tried to take an apple from its hand. Of course, the king couldn't resist anything mechanical…'

'Like Daddy?'

'Like Daddy, yes. But Finella had tampered with the arrows. As soon as the king picked up the apple, an arrow pierced him through the heart and he dropped down DEAD!'

I jump, even though I've heard all this before. 'And she RAN and she RAN!'

'She did!' Mum leaps up, play-acting now, leaves crackling beneath her feet. 'The king is bleeding all over the place and the servants are hammering at the door!'

I jump up too. 'Run, Finella! Get out of there!'

'And Finella slips through a hidden tunnel and runs, and keeps on running, dodging the king's men-at-arms. She leads them a dance across the Howe of the Mearns, over the hill which now bears her name, Strath Finella, and here to this deep, dark gully. She's a woman of the woods – she knows when to hide and when to break cover…'

Mum is dancing now, through the bracken and heather, and I'm skipping after her. I can hear hounds whining, men shouting. Mum stops for dramatic effect within sight of the waterfall.

The tremendous thunder of it enters our hearts and snatches away our voices.

'They say she took to the trees, walking across the tops of them to escape.'

'Could she have? Was she magic?'

'Who knows what you can do when you need to escape the inescapable? And then she came to the waterfall.'

'Uh oh. Time for Plan B,' I whisper.

Mum takes a step closer to the edge of the falls. Stares straight ahead, hands on hips like a warrior queen. Beyond her there is only nothingness and wet mist. When she glances back at me, the storytelling buzz has left her and her face is in shadow. There are dark mysteries in her eyes which I don't understand. 'At the end, she had no choice. It was jump or be killed.'

'Do you think she survived?'

Mum stoops to brush the hair away from my face. 'What do you think?'

1

Two Days After

The bus brakes at the end of our drive. Hefting the rucksack onto my shoulder, I get ready to jump. So many buses, so many stops in the last couple of years, never knowing where my boots will land: tarmac, mud, sand, flood.

A single phone call from halfway across the world was all it took to bring me home. *Ellie, something bad has happened.*

As the bus pulls away in a fug of diesel, I'm left staring at the house: mossy green roof blending with the trees and the hedge running riot. It's doubled in size since my last visit. The only sign of life is a lone crow perched on the chimney. It eyes me with suspicion.

The scent of leftover bus fumes makes me feel sick. Hitching my rucksack higher, I begin the familiar trudge. The drive has been carved up by an endless procession of vehicles en route to the scrapyard behind the house. For most of them, this is a one-way street, and they've left unwilling claw-marks in the surface – deep ruts brimming with rainbow-coloured water. Even the trees have grown wild in my absence, holding hands above my head like playmates. 'The Grand Old Duke of York'. I am six again, jumping off the school bus with my Polly Pocket book bag, picking up a stick to beat the rain from the branches. I was always the kid with the longest stick, the grubbiest shirt, the biggest mouth. The kid from the scrapyard.

It's been two years since I last walked down this drive. Then, Mum had tied balloons to the gate and was waiting for me with a big hug. But not today. Not today.

Today, there is a police van in the yard.

I let myself in the back door. It's like falling through a hole in time, with all the usual suspects sitting round the table: my father, River, Shelby Smith. The teatime smell of cucumber and tinned salmon makes my stomach cramp. Unable to face airline food, I've flown nearly 6000 miles fuelled by only water and crisps.

My father is buttering a slice of white bread, wiping his knife compulsively on the side of his plate as he always does. He stops, mid wipe, when he sees me and remains very still. River gets up in slow motion, comes to engulf me in a bear hug that blocks out everything else. He's taller than me now, with muscles of iron. He lets go eventually, leaving me smelling of some cheap teen cologne. There's a new sharpness to his face, his eyes.

I shed my rucksack and sink into a chair. River gets a mug from the dresser and pours tea. My father still hasn't moved. He rubs his silver beard, but it's Shelby, the adopted Rook, who reaches over to grasp my hand.

'Tell me again.' I've barely spoken to anyone in twenty-four hours and my voice comes out all croaky. 'Tell me what happened.'

'It was an accident,' River says.

He's still standing there with the teapot, beside our mother's empty chair, and he looks so like her – that hesitant stance, the way he hides behind a shock of dark hair. I rise and take the teapot from him.

'Go on. It's okay. Tell me everything. You were at the Den of Finella?'

I replace the teapot carefully on its iron trivet.

'We'd gone for a walk, Mum and me. How many times have we done that? I – I was standing right next to her, at the top of the waterfall.' I nod slowly, rub his bony shoulder as if to ease the words out of him. 'I didn't actually see what happened. I turned away for a second and she must have slipped somehow. I heard her cry out and then—' His eyes are fixed on the floor tiles.

'What? What did you see?'

He looks up, but his gaze flinches from mine. 'I didn't see anything after that. She was just – *gone*. I didn't have my phone, so I ran back and got Dad and Shelby and Offshore Dave, and Julie called the police.'

'We drove along to the bridge. It was quicker,' Dad says. He looks at Shelby, but Shelby is studying his plate.

'And? Did you see any sign of her? Did you go down to the bottom?' My patience is slipping.

'The police did. They sent divers upstream from the beach end.' My father's voice cracks. He's rubbing his beard in little frantic movements. 'The coastguard, search and rescue helicopters – all there within minutes, really. But no sign of her. There's been no sign.' The last bit is a whisper. It hangs heavy in the air.

At the end of the table, Shelby hasn't uttered a word. He and my mother are of the same clan. They come from a world of fairgrounds, where folk keep things in the family. Shelby followed her up north, claiming to be 'just passing through'. The reality is he has nowhere else to go. He reaches for his dusty black fedora and jams it onto his head.

'I'll be getting back then, boss.'

We all know he's going no further than the caravan across the yard, but we mumble our goodbyes. Although it's a Thursday, he's wearing his Sunday-best shirt under his denim jacket – stripes of blue and gold, like a seaside deck chair.

'Ellie . . . I'm sorry. We'll talk later, my love.'

I nod, watch his departing back. Shelby has been so much a part of my life it's hard to see where kinship ends and blood ties begin.

'So what do we do now?'

'We wait.' My father looks at me, dry-eyed.

'Not fucking likely.' I slip my iPhone from my bag. 'I didn't come all this way to sit and wait.'

'She's dead. Your mother's dead. It's a sixty-foot drop, with rocks at the bottom, and she couldn't swim. How could she have survived?'

'You can't say that! It's too soon. Maybe she's stuck somewhere. There are caves all along the coast. Remember the legend. No one knows if Finella survived when she jumped over the waterfall.'

My father rolls his eyes. 'Bollocks. That's nothing more than a fairy story!'

River droops over the table, buries his face in his arms. I want to argue, but I feel drained. I turn to my mobile, scroll through a ton of enquiries on my Facebook feed. Someone has posted a link to some local headlines: MOTHER OF TWO MISSING PRESUMED DROWNED AT ABERDEENSHIRE BEAUTY SPOT. Countless questions. *Is this your mum, Ellie? We're all thinking about you. Are you home? Ellie – get in touch!*

I click back to my home screen. There are text messages too. I cannot deal with this right now. Dad reaches over and snatches the mobile. A sudden gust of memory chills me: my old Nokia; my father hurling the device against the wall. My heart smashing into a million pieces.

'We'll keep this between ourselves, as we always do.' He places the mobile in the centre of the table, beside the plate of leftover sandwiches.

River raises his head. I hadn't noticed how red his eyes are. 'We'll need to post a picture on Facebook,' he says, 'and write something nice. A memorial. You're good at that, Ellie.'

'Not yet! What is wrong with you?' I glare at each of them in turn. My father glares back; River picks his grimy nails. 'We need to organise a search party, ask for help.'

'What do you think the police are doing?' Dad snaps. 'Let them do their job. The house has been full of folk since it happened. Last night we had Julie and her family – and Offshore Dave, the Duthies. Some dame from the village who brought enough soup to feed an army.'

River nods. 'We stayed up all night.'

'I need to do *something*.' I get to my feet. 'I'm going to the den. I just need to be there.'

'Don't be ridiculous. What can you do? Nothing.'

I ignore Dad and look to my brother for support. 'Come with me, River.'

'No!' Dad slaps his palm down on the table. 'The light's fading. We don't want another accident.'

'Whatever. I'll go on my own.'

'Ellie!'

I unlace my boots and toss them aside. Mum's wellies are waiting at the door. I put them on.

2

Outside, everything reminds me of my mother.

I walk as if my limbs are frozen, as if a wrong step might dislodge the frost. Past the police van and Shelby's immaculate, green-painted caravan, curtains drawn against unwanted intrusion. There's an unmistakeable scent of bacon. I slow down, spend way too long deliberating over whether it's a just-cooked sort of smell or a days-old lingering one, and trying not to judge him on it.

Somewhere on the caravan are my mother's initials. She helped him paint the gold and red curlicues and fleur-de-lis, the loopy fairground lettering between the windows: 'Value & Civility'. Her initials, I. S. R. – Imelda Smith Rook – are hidden there somewhere, but I am too fragile to look. I am an icicle, waiting to snap.

I remember the morning Shelby towed his caravan into the yard. I must have been about twelve; River was still a toddler, clutching my hand. The caravan's curtained windows were heavy-lidded, giving nothing away. Handfuls of grass festooned the undercarriage, as if the vehicle had been pulled free from a place where it shouldn't have been. All the men came from the yard to witness this strange spectacle, and there was a lot of banter, a lot of revving and general kicking of tyres. I've noticed guys do that a lot when faced with a strange vehicle, as if they need to put their mark on it. Kicking is more civilised than pissing, I guess.

When I think of that time, I remember my mother's expression. She never ever looked like that, all lit up from the inside. Shelby Smith was the closest thing she had to family, a distant cousin many times removed. He brought a blast of fresh Nottingham air to the Aberdeenshire coast, I suppose. It turned back time for a small while. Made her sparkle.

His hair was dark back then, the hat less dusty. I can still see him sliding out of his Land Rover to plant a kiss on my mother's cheek. I was fascinated by the faded denim jacket, the single gold earring. We had a campfire in the yard that night. The men got legless on cheap lager and Shelby played some old tunes on a battered melodeon. River fell asleep against my shoulder and turned all rosy in the firelight. It was a good night.

Despite his claim to be 'just passing through', Shelby's caravan hasn't moved since. When was that? I try to calculate. Thirteen or fourteen years ago. I'm not sure when we realised his wheels were down for good. Maybe when Mum went out with her paint pots and covered all the dents and scrapes with roses and oak leaves and curlicues. Mum was good at covering things up: shabby paintwork, stained school shirts. Bruises.

I make my way along the steel palisade behind Shelby's colourful caravan, the fearsome electric gate, with its spikes and security cameras. Beyond it, the mechanical grabber rears up like some stalky steampunk heron, neck arched, getting ready to pounce. The place is closed, given the circumstances; the only movement is the black flap of the crows in the car stacks. They caw and fight like gulls on a cliff face. My mother likes to talk to the crows.

Where the fence ends, the wilderness begins. My father fancies himself as some kind of scrap baron. Lawler Rook, King of the Scrappies. He tries to make out the den is part of his little kingdom, but it's not his. It's not the sort of place that can be possessed. It has its own agenda. If he fancies himself as a king, then my mother is the Queen of the Woods. It's my mother's place. She took the time to learn its language.

The trees get bigger the deeper you go: oaks with thick trunks and leaves drooping like prayer flags; silver birches with bark so thin and papery you can touch the new skin beneath. I stride out in my mother's wellies, placing my feet where she must have placed hers on that last walk. How many days ago? How many hours? I try to do the maths, attempting to quantify the amount of time I have been, to all intents and purposes, motherless, but jet lag and exhaustion make me fuzzy. I give up and slither to the ground at the base of a broad oak. My heart is thumping all the way through my body, an alien drumbeat. In an instant, our tight-knit, isolated little world has turned upside down. Everyone will have a way of coping, an opinion, a plan. But what happens next is up to me.

3

Three Days After

I sit bolt upright, head swimming with sleep, fingers clutching the duvet, as if my bed is adrift and I need to be anchored. The wardrobe, the rose-patterned wallpaper – all so familiar. I check the floor. My rucksack is there, spewing clothes across the carpet. My mother's wellies, one upright, one collapsed on its side, are caked in mud.

Butterfly fragments of a dream spin out of reach. I close my eyes, shut down my breathing. Wait. Trees, skinny and bare, their branches low-set like eyebrows, pulling at my clothes. Fallen things smothered with old growth – moss and fungi I can't name. Coarse, dead grass. Air that tastes of earth and rust and mouldy upholstery.

I come to a place in the woods where the sound of my own footsteps disappears. A row of rusty car skeletons, painted with moss; rough grass and briars growing up through them. Empty eye sockets – gaping holes where their doors and windscreens should be. Seats shredded by foxes. Some of them list drunkenly, others bear the battle scars of old accidents. Look closer and you'll see bird shit on the dashboards, mice's nests in the gloveboxes.

But I don't want to get that close.

With a gasp I come fully awake, scramble out of bed as if that too is tainted by the nightmare. I stumble over the wellies, stare at them as if I don't know them any more. I throw on my old dressing gown and pad downstairs. River is already in the kitchen, plugged into his phone, making toast. I can hear the thump of a bass track, and I have to tap him on the shoulder to get his attention. He pulls out one earbud, but even then I have to repeat my question twice.

'What was she wearing – Mum? Did she have a coat on? Boots?'

He blinks at me, unsmiling. 'What does it matter?'

'What did you tell the police?'

He sighs. 'She was wearing a coat. Green, I think. The one with the little white flowers on it. And a thingy . . .' He gestures to his neck. 'A scarf. The red one with the birds on it.'

'Owls.'

'Yeah. Them.'

He goes back to buttering his toast, but something else has been bothering me.

'Wasn't it Tuesday, when it happened?'

'So?'

He's making such a mess. I set about clearing up, banging things around, although there's no one here to care. I imagine Mum telling me to be careful with her good plates.

'So why were you not at school? Why were you walking with Mum in the middle of the day?'

River shrugs, pushes his earbuds in deeper and goes searching for his boots, toast in hand, leaving a trail of crumbs from the toaster to the back door. The boots are on a folded newspaper, where I put them after he'd abandoned them under the table the night before. He scuffs back in his socks, which may once have been white. I have a mental image of his room: curtains still drawn, unidentifiable heaps of dirty washing all around the bed. Who's going to sort that out now?

'You're dripping marmalade all over the place. Get a bloody plate.'

I give him a hefty whack across the arm and my fingers come away stinging. He's going on sixteen, but he seems to have sprouted into a man. Last time I was home, he still had that little-boy look about him, but I suppose you have to grow up fast round here.

'It was an in-service day.'

He plonks himself onto a chair and shoves his enormous feet into workman's boots. He must be a size nine. I'm not sure I believe him about the in-service day, but his boots are leaving treads of dried mud on the floor, so I go and get the sweeping brush. It occupies my mind.

'So where are you going now?'

'Well, I'm not going to school. You get a week off for a parent.'

'River!'

'It's true. I don't mean anything by it. And anyway, the police lady says there'll be a lot of media attention, and we should keep a low profile.'

I regret sounding so shocked. Moving close to him, I ruffle his hair. He smells of shampoo.

'So where—?'

'Stonehaven, with Dad. There's a car he wants to see. A vintage Daimler.'

'Doesn't that seem a bit … callous? Even for Dad?'

'It's his way of coping, I guess. Business as usual.'

Business as usual. This family has always been about business. I should know that by now.

'But you can't leave me here to deal with stuff.' Something breaks loose in me, skitters through my innards. 'I don't know what to do. How to handle . . . *this*.'

'The yard's closed.'

'Not *that*! This other stuff. Police stuff. They'll be sniffing around and—'

'We don't have a body.' River's voice is gruff, too grown-up. 'There's nothing anyone can do. We'll only be half an hour. The police lady – the family whatsit cop – she was here before. She might come back. She left a load of leaflets and shit.'

He nods towards the table, where a small stash of papers sits under a blue-striped milk jug. Shuffling his boots, River stands up, giving my elbow an affectionate dunt. 'People deal with things in their own way. Dad needs to get away from here for a bit.'

With River gone, I stand in the empty kitchen for a long time, listening to the steady drip of the tap and the distant barking of a dog, before sinking into the nearest chair. Last night's sandwiches are curling on the plate and the smell makes me want to heave. I push them away and sit with my face in my hands for a long time, and when I finally look up, all I can see are the leaflets River mentioned, poking out from under the milk jug.

Very slowly, I ease them out. They are basic, factual, printed on pastel-coloured paper, with line drawings of the recently bereaved. One of them talks about funerals and pensions. None of them reflect what is happening to us. They fail to mention dirty laundry, or food shopping, or skipping school. Fear burns through my gullet like acid. I pick up a clutch of business cards. 'PC Lorraine Sampson. Family Liaison.'

It doesn't seem to have anything to do with me. I set about crumbling the leftovers into small pieces for the birds. Mum always does that. She likes the sparrows and the blackbirds and the wrens, but most of all she likes to feed the crows. So I tear the bread into little bits, fingers greasy with salmon and butter. Who will feed the crows now? The leaflets don't have an answer.

Being home brings up all manner of forgotten things. My mother is the thread that connects me to my childhood. Even when I'm far away, she updates me regularly on neighbourhood gossip and the goings-on of people I went to school with. She was the first to tell me that Liam Duthie had broken up with Katie Coutts last year, even before Liam changed his status on Facebook. I think I punched the air – not because I harboured any ambition to rekindle an old flame, but because Katie Coutts had it coming.

It's strange, the way old grudges slumber away under a rock, until someone pokes them with a stick. When I think of Shore Road Primary now, it brings back that sick, awkward feeling of first-day nerves. I didn't like the newness, the strange smells. The *bigness* of it all. It wasn't an outside bigness, like the yard or the woods, but a closed-in bigness, with no promise of escape. They slammed the doors on us, shut out the sea and the sky and the screaming gulls. I was a feisty kid. I'm surprised they could keep me contained in that little classroom. My first day at school was a catastrophe, although I remember it now with something like amusement.

When the paints come out in the afternoon – bright, solid greens and blues – a thrill of hope makes me leap from my red plastic chair. I will paint home! I hunch over the table, serious and scowling, working the paint with a stiff, stubby brush into something I can recognise. And then Katie Coutts ruins it. Poisonous little Katie Coutts, only five years old. She comes up behind me and deliberately spills her dirty water all over my picture. It's an accident, she says, but rage and homesickness boil up in me like scarlet paint, and I burst into tears. Mrs Cargill is there in an instant, but I can barely spit out my objections between sobs.

'What were you painting, Ellie?'

'It's a' – *sniff* – 'WATERFALL!'

'Oh well then.' Mrs Cargill pats my head. 'A little extra water won't do any harm.'

The casual injustice stabs me in the heart. I glare at Katie so hard she flinches, but that isn't enough. I'm so mad I need more. The only ammunition within reach is the colourful words Offshore Dave hurls about the yard. I know them all, so I pick the ones I like best and fire. I can still hear the echo of them, like an arrow, arcing past the scandalised noses of Mrs Cargill and the teaching assistant.

'Katie, you're a fuckin' cunt!'

4

Out in the yard, I find Mum's battered little blue Fiesta, tucked in between the giant tow truck and Shelby's ancient Land Rover Defender. The police van is gone, leaving the little car exposed. Dad's Range Rover – current model and so white he has to wash it every day – is absent, of course, purring its way to Stonehaven as if none of this matters. All that's left is the faint stink of fuel. I'm jealous of my father's ability to hold on to the threads of his own life while mine are unravelling. I'm angry, too. Raging at him – and yes, raging at my mother. Three days ago, I was sipping rum from a coconut in Hanoi. It's not fair. None of this is bloody fair.

The Fiesta is locked, so I peer through the side window, shielding my eyes and pressing close. The interior is empty of anything personal – not a scarf, or a shopping list, or loose change. It's parked up all wrong, as if Mum had had it in mind to sneak back out at some point and straighten it up before Dad had a chance to complain. My father is a man of straight lines. He never got her curlicues.

There's movement in Shelby's caravan, a faint rumbling and rocking, and the man himself appears. He looks unwashed and washed out. He sees me but doesn't speak, slumps down on the caravan step to light his roll-up. Smoke is soon curling from beneath the black fedora. I go and stand in front of him, so he can't ignore me. He takes a slow drag of his cigarette and slants his gaze at me, still saying nothing.

'Hey.' I flip the brim of his hat with two fingers and it tumbles to the ground. His iron-grey hair is tied with a bootlace and his scalp looks oddly vulnerable, the hair flattened and pink skin showing through in patches, like one of the silver birches in the woods. He makes no effort to pick up the hat, just narrows his eyes at me some more.

'Be careful with that. Got that hat from—'

'A banjo player in Nebraska. I know. I know all your stories, Shel. You'll have to come up with some more.'

He smiles a bit. 'Mebbe I will. Mebbe so. How are you doing, my love?' He's looking at the ground, not at me, but the air between us is suddenly tense.

'I don't know. I really don't.'

'One day at a time. That's all we can do.'

'I feel like I'm holding my breath. All the time.' I shake my head miserably. 'How are you?'

'Holding the line.' He squints up at me, eyes the same green as the van. As long as I've known him, he's been a chameleon, still and quiet and ready to run. 'You went to the den last night? What did you see?'

I'm not sure what he wants to hear.

I pick up his hat, dust it off and plant it back on his head. 'What would you expect me to see? Nothing. There were more cops on the bridge, but I stayed down low and followed the bank. I couldn't hear anything but the roar of the water. I couldn't see anything disturbed at the edge, no skid marks in the mud, no rocks disturbed. No sign that she was there at all.'

'What were the rozzers doing?'

'How would I know? Sitting in their van eating doughnuts, maybe.'

He doesn't answer, just nods in the direction of the back door. 'You got a visitor, my love.'

I look where he's looking, towards a young woman with a black folder in her hand. Although she's hatless, her fair hair tied back severely, she's unmistakeably a cop. My heart sinks.

'Jesus, does this look kind of official to you?' I glance back,

15

but Shelby has already nipped his fag and ducked into the caravan. Question answered.

'Lorraine Sampson, Family Liaison. I thought I'd touch base with you. You must be Ellie?'

The newcomer's hand in mine is freezing. She makes some comment about the weather and I invite her in, pull out a chair at the table for her.

'Tea?' I ask.

She shakes her head, and then gets straight to it. 'There's nothing new to report,' she says. 'The search is ongoing and we're still checking the coastline.'

'There are caves. Along the coast.' I'm sitting opposite her, squeezing my hands together like I'm praying.

She looks at me with professional, weary compassion. 'As I explained to your father – where is he, by the way? Are you here on your own?'

'He's gone out' – I catch sight of the blue-striped jug – 'for milk. He's taken my brother with him. Just to get out of the house for a while.'

'Yes, of course.'

I catch her looking at the plate of scraps and feel the need to explain that too. 'My mother likes to feed the crows.'

Lorraine's smile flickers and fades. She makes deliberate eye contact. 'Ellie. While this is still being treated as a missing person investigation, the fact that your brother witnessed your mother's fall means that the chances of a positive outcome are not good. Do you understand that?' My heart ticks to a stop. She rattles on. 'As I explained to your father, the more time a casualty spends in the water, with no sighting of them, the less chance there is of a positive outcome. Your brother states that he didn't see your mum after she fell, and our general guideline is that after this much time in the water . . . I have to be honest with you, Ellie. There's no—'

'Yes. Yes, I get it.' I spring up from my seat, gather up the plate of bird food and stand there with it clutched to my ribs, refusing to look at her. She takes the hint. I hear her sigh, and three more business cards appear on the table.

'That's my number. You can call me at any time, Ellie, and I'll get you whatever help you need.'

She gets up to leave and I know she'll be straight on the phone to whatever agencies produce those pastel-green leaflets. Whatever. I'll make sure I'm out when they call.

5

Four Days After

Another morning after another restless night, and daylight finds me sitting on the side of my bed, googling 'what happens after a death' and 'seven stages of grief'. I make a brief, chilly visit to the bathroom and pull on yesterday's clothes. The stairs lead down into the front hall, and I pause for a moment, hearing the dull rumble of voices beyond the closed kitchen door. I don't particularly want to see Dad or River; I just want to be alone with my thoughts. Quickly, before I change my mind and volunteer for breakfast duties, I let myself out the front door.

The front garden runs parallel to the drive, screened from it by a mass of unruly privet. There's evidence of a genteel past: a path of herringbone brick leading to the road; a rusty Victorian gate. I suppose there were borders here once, with hollyhocks and roses, but coarse grass has taken over and the plants manage as best they can. Springtime is coming slowly – a lone red tulip pushing its way through the wilderness and a stubborn clump of bluebells in the far corner.

There's a green-painted bench just outside the door, where Mum sits in good weather. She calls the garden her sanctuary, a place where she can go to avoid the mountains of scrap, but you can't dodge the death rattle of doomed vehicles beyond the hedge, or the film of fuel that clogs your throat. There is no escape either from the things that Dad thinks are 'worth a bob or two'. Mum has done her best to upcycle them. Old coal scuttles, weighing scales and tractor seats, all painted glossy black and studded with flowers. Her initials are on the back of each piece, as if she fears being anonymous.

I plonk myself down on the bench, beside a clutch of pebbles and shells and a handful of sea glass. My mother is a jackdaw, a collector of sparkle and colour. All her favourites are here: blues, greens, china white, like chinks of sunshine on water. There's a cushion here too, made of crocheted squares. I hug the cushion to me and sniff, but it only smells of damp, not of her. I feel like she's just out of sight, maybe gone to the shop, or for a walk.

My pilgrimage to the waterfall is still playing on a loop in my head. I close my eyes.

There were police on the bridge, at least two of them, standing beside a big white van. I could hear static as they talked on their radios, but the sound of rushing water was so loud that I couldn't make out the words. As I slipped past, I noticed that one of them was holding a bunch of flowers. Of course there'd be flowers. This new truth hit me like a dart. I've seen it on the telly often enough – people leaving bouquets at the scene of a tragedy, propped up in cellophane shrouds, handwritten cards gushing all sorts of crap about someone they never really knew.

I kept low beneath the parapet of the bridge, so no one could see me. Far below, the water was a cauldron of foaming white. I stuck to the path like glue as it snaked between the trees. The edge of the gully has eroded in places, and you have to step with great care over tree roots, avoiding the slippery bits. It's treacherous, but Mum knew that. She'd always known it. The nearer you get to the waterfall, the more dangerous it becomes.

I negotiated the path, placing one foot in front of the other. Baby steps. It had been raining and the going was mucky, but I took my time. I knew which bits to avoid. I remembered the parts that have slipped away into nothingness, where you have to clamber up onto the slope, holding on to the tree trunks, working your way round like a commando. To drop your gaze is fatal. The dizzying depths of the flooded gorge will stop you in your tracks. Don't look down, Mum used to tell us. Don't look down.

There's a point where the path ends, and a tributary, hurtling through the fields from the south, tumbles into the gully in a haze of thunder and spray. Finella's waterfall. The path evolves into a ledge of sorts, which some long-dead Victorian decided would make a splendid viewing platform. Most of the dressed stone has long since collapsed into the abyss. There is nothing between you and the spitting water, and if you lean over, you can see the messy confluence of the two rivers, sixty feet below. But who would want to go that close?

I imagine the jump, the river closing over me. Water in my nose, my mouth, stopping my breath . . . Panic jerks me back to the present. I'm still sitting on the bench in the garden, my ears filled with birdsong. The hedge is alive with sparrows and the crows are waiting in the pear tree.

My mother has been in the newspaper only twice in her life. The first time, she was campaigning against council budget cuts. I must have been around nine or ten, because it was before River, although when her photo was splashed all over the *Gazette*, there was the suspicion of a bump under her peasant top. There she was, one hand on the remains of the Victorian wall, the spray from Finella's waterfall stippling the background.

She wanted the council to upgrade the paths around the Den of Finella. I think Dad's nagging had spurred her into action. He'd tried to ban us all from the den, but in a rare act of defiance, Mum continued to take us there. She swore us to secrecy, made us shake on it, spitting on our hands and everything, like real showmen. Everyone knows that's binding. We're good at keeping secrets. Treacherous, Dad had declared. One day, someone will fall to their death.

I don't remember much about the photo shoot. A guy in a thin jacket that smelled of pies. A few slick phrases: *Fluff the hair up a bit, hon. Tilt your head. Where's that lovely smile?* I remember Dad being furious when he opened the paper. What was this? The Rooks plastered all over the press? She tried to explain that she hadn't really wanted her photograph taken, but he wouldn't listen. I'm not sure what happened after that, but there was a horrible atmosphere about the place for ages, and Mum never went public with her thoughts again.

And now that same photograph has resurfaced.

I hear voices on the road. Still clutching the damp cushion, I get up from the bench and sleepwalk to the gate. I recognise Sharon Duthie's voice. The other one is younger, and very determined.

'Give that back, Mrs Duthie!' The paperboy snatches the *Gazette* from the woman's hands. 'You'll get me into trouble. They always get the *Gazette*. Auld mannie Rook'll be phonin' my boss if he doesnae get his paper. And anyway, that's censorship.'

'Censor, my arse!' There's a brief tussle. Sharon raises her walking stick, and then they both spot me, standing there at the gate. The paperboy gives up and walks his bike away, muttering darkly, as Sharon folds the newspaper and tries to hide it.

'Ellie!' Her voice is sharp with embarrassment. She's still in her dressing gown, an unflattering yellow that clashes with her auburn bob and pink cheeks. I look past her, to her white bungalow on the other side of the road. In the triangle between the gable end and the garage, I can see the North Sea.

Leaning heavily on the walking stick, her gaze drops to the paper in her hand. 'I – I just didn't want you to see it.'

I've already seen it. Even upside down, the headline screams at me.

TRAGEDY AT LOCAL BEAUTY SPOT

The sea is the colour of pencil lead. It looks so, so cold.

A hand brushes mine. 'Ellie, are you okay, lass?'

Anything washed downstream ends up there, in the leaden North Sea. I let my gaze sink back to Sharon, and I say the first thing that comes into my head.

'Cold water carries heat away from the body twenty-five times faster than air of the same temperature.'

I'd tucked the newspaper under my arm and refused Sharon's offer of a cuppa. Warning bells always go off when I see Sharon. She has ailments I've no intention of asking about and eyes the colour of fudge, which suck people in. My mother was a captive audience, but right now I don't have time for her drama. Besides, she reminds me too much of her son.

'Pop over later then,' Sharon had said. 'You know Liam's back home? Like a bloody boomerang. Ach, I never liked Katie anyway. Ellie, what am I thinking? Away you go in. I just didn't want you to . . .' She took a breath and I could sense a loaded question looming. 'They're saying she just lost her footing.' A huge sniff, crumpled tissue to the nose, and those fudge-brown eyes as sharp as pins. 'Is that what happened, lass?'

I brushed her away. 'That's what they're saying. I wasn't here.'

'Are you sure it was an accident, hen?'

I'd already turned to go, but this stopped me in my tracks. The saliva dried in my mouth. 'What do you mean by that?'

She reached for my hand, but both of mine were taken up with the cushion and the paper, so she just squeezed my wrist awkwardly. 'She'd been a wee bit down lately, what with River playing up.' Her fingers had teased through the cluster of beach bracelets on my arm. I pulled away abruptly. 'My depression – I've never hidden it from anyone. I'm an open book, as you know, but your mum was good at hiding things. I spotted her crying the other day. She tried to hide it, but I could tell.'

I'd had to prise my teeth apart. 'So what are you saying? That she wanted to drown?'

Sharon held up her hands, and her yellow fleecy dressing gown gaped at the bosom.

'I'm just saying – maybe she was depressed. River was with her, wasn't he? Even though it was a school day?'

I'd already turned to go, barging through the old gate with such force it shuddered on its hinges. 'My mother was fine. I'd have known.'

Her voice followed me up the garden path. 'But like you say, you weren't here.'

6

My mother tidied me away long ago. When I lived here, my bedroom resembled River's, all clothes mountains and cereal bowls under the bed. Now, I can only find myself in the dust on top of the wardrobe.

There's an old suitcase of my grandmother's up there that contains all the bits of me my mother thinks she should keep: school jotters with gold stars, concert tickets, diaries, old copies of *Seventeen*. I have to stand on a chair to drag it down. Hefting it onto the bed, springing the old-fashioned latches to slowly lift the lid, the empty smell of nostalgia hits me like a pain.

My scrapbook is right at the bottom, tucked beneath an envelope of faded black-and-white photos (Grandma Rook's) and my yellow Brownie cap, a small thumbprint on its peak. Alongside it is the sash with all its badges. Arts and crafts, first aid, culture – I liked that one. I'd cooked haggis, neeps and tatties and told my unit about the legend of Finella.

I sink down on the bed. I have a silly urge to put the cap on, but instead, I pick it up and examine it, turning it over and over as if it will transport me somewhere else.

I'm seven and all eyes are on me. A ring of fidgety, cross-legged little girls and Brown Owl smiling from the sidelines. I'd tried to explain to my mother that morning how I felt, but she'd said everyone gets butterflies, even big people. You've just got to swallow them down and get on with it. I swallow and open my mouth and pray that the butterflies won't stifle my voice.

'So there was a warrior princess called Finella and she lived in Aberdeenshire in the year 995.' I have them at *princess*. Eight pairs of eyes widen, and I press on, ramping up the drama. 'She lived not far from here, actually, and she had a son. She loved him very much, but he was a rebel . . .'

'What's a revel?' says Katie Coutts, her thumb in her mouth.

'It means you don't like being told what to do.' I glare at her for interrupting my story. 'Anyway, he plotted against King Kenneth, and the king said that the boy had to be hexecuted and Finella got as mad as anything. She was a hunter, so she had lots of weapons.'

'What did she hunt?' asks another girl, like it matters.

'I dunno. Deer, maybe.'

'Aw, I like deer.' Katie again.

'It doesn't *matter*. Finella lured the king to her castle and shot him with a crossbow.'

'Ewww!' My fellow Brownies screw up their noses. A certain power steals over me and the butterfly wings fade in my throat.

'Yes, she shot him and there was blood everywhere. Pouring out of him.'

Our leader coughs, and I take the hint. 'Yeah, so the king's men came after her and chased her through the glens.'

'Was she on a horse?'

'No, she—'

'Maybe someone gave her a lift in a getaway car.'

'No!' Tears spring to my eyes. I knew they wouldn't listen. I hadn't even remembered the gruesome part that Mum told me about the statue and the apple. Brown Owl stirs.

'What a lovely story, Ellie. Well done. Big round of applause.' She begins clapping like a seal and the girls join in.

I flop down beside Katie Coutts. I never even got to the good bit, where Finella bravely leaps from the waterfall to escape. Katie Coutts leans towards me, breathing sickly Ribena fumes. 'You have dirt on your cap,' she says.

Now, I pick up the yellow cap, place my grown-up thumb on the oily mark. Sometimes you just don't get to say the things you want to say.

What I'm really looking for is loose in the scrapbook. A newspaper cutting from the time before. It's gone yellow with age, but that same image of my mother stares out at me. She is young, defiant. Real. I wish I'd taken more time to get to know this woman. Sharon was right – I wasn't here. I should have been. I should have seen what was happening, and come home sooner.

I flatten out today's paper and place the cutting alongside it on the bed. TRAGEDY AT LOCAL BEAUTY SPOT. I trace a finger along the outline of my mother's body, then I fold both pictures into one neat package and stow them away in Grandma Rook's suitcase. No point in getting Dad all worked up about it.

7

Six Days After

By Monday, the yard is open for business.

The words hover unspoken around the breakfast table: *too soon*. My jaw is set as I fry bacon and eggs for my father and Shelby and River. Mum's absence is there when I can't find the old black pan. It's there when I spill hot oil on my flip-flops and burn my toes, and when the egg yolks burst. It's very much there when my father assesses his plate without comment.

'Beautiful that, my love.' Shelby winks and hangs his hat on the back of his chair.

'Dad's mustard.' River widens his eyes at me like I'm missing a trick, inclines his head towards the dresser. Oh yes, the mustard. He has it at every meal – a fiery concoction he mixes himself and keeps in a little glass Colman's pot. The pot is stored in the dresser, to be offered up on a vintage saucer with a dainty silver spoon. Sighing, I head for the dresser.

Afterwards, I follow the men outside, my feet stuffed once again into Mum's daisy-print wellies. The huge steel gate is open for the first time since the accident. That iron bird still has its beak to the ground, and there's an inky black crow perched on the highest part of it. I expect they're both in the mood for carrion.

Shelby reckons that people remind him of vehicles. He's got a point. Mum's little Fiesta is crowded out by tougher, newer vehicles: a filthy white Hyundai van and a smart lilac Mini.

A bicycle that looks like it's been rescued from a skip is chained to the railings. I know what I'll see in the white van: piles of fast-food wrappers and yellowing copies of *The Sun*. The wedge between the dashboard and the windscreen will be stuffed with everything Offshore Dave needs most in his life. He calls it his filing system. Dave's fluorescent boiler suit, too, is crammed with invoices, receipts and empty fag packets. His face, like the vehicle, is a stranger to water. I suspect he goes through the motions with a heavy-duty garage wipe, but you could grow potatoes in his crow's feet.

I peep in the window of the white van. From nowhere, an explosion of barking makes me jump. I'd forgotten the Guardians of the Van – Bill and Bono, two German shepherds, with sharp teeth and wet jowls. The glass is filthy with new spittle and old smears, and the whole cab is rocking with the power of their fury. I back away and the commotion subsides.

I don't expect them to recognise me. They'd arrived as puppies, not long before I left on my travels – I think Dave had acquired them in lieu of some gambling debt – and they became part of the yard fixtures. At first, we all gave in to some serious puppy-cuddling, until one of them peed on the kitchen floor and Dad beat it with a rolled-up newspaper. Mum wouldn't let them into the house after that – not to protect the floor, but to protect them. Dave left them to patrol the yard at night and they stayed in the van during the day. He took them home at weekends, and occasionally for a walk, but he has turned them into stereotypical junkyard dogs. No one remembers now which is Bill and which is Bono. They wear studded collars and stink of shit and old oil; like Dave, they've never been troubled by shampoo.

The little Mini, by comparison, belongs to Julie, who does the accounts. She wears short skirts and black tights and complains about the cold a lot. She colour-coordinates her eyes, nails and handbags, but isn't scared to out-man the men when the need arises.

I spend a few minutes staring at the bike. There's a loop of seaweed hanging from the frame.

Shelby comes up behind me.

'Another day, another dollar.' He slaps a large spanner against his palm.

I make a face. 'It's too soon. Don't you think it's too soon? It's like he doesn't care.'

'He cares. He cares too much, that's the problem.'

His eyes meet mine for a moment, and then I turn and enter the yard for the first time in years.

Julie is already making herself at home in her Portacabin world. I slouch in the doorway and watch her switch everything on in order of importance: electric heater, overhead light, kettle, computer. She turns and spots me lurking, and suddenly I'm squashed against her purple leather jacket, trying not to breathe in last night's perfume and artisan gin.

'Och, Ellie.' She holds me away, squashes me some more. 'Ellie.'

I wriggle away out of reach, blinking in the artificial light. The Portacabin has only one small window overlooking the yard, and that's partially covered in promotional stickers from various oil companies. Someone's made a half-hearted attempt to pick them off. Probably Julie, with her gel manicure.

'Any news?' She's regarding me in that nervous way people do when they don't know how you're going to react – head on one side, teeth pinching her glossy lower lip.

I shake my head, stare at the corkboard on the wall behind her. Loads of invoices and memos speared with coloured pins. And photos: Christmas drinks at the local; Julie's cats; Julie and her husband on holiday somewhere hot and sunny.

Julie supresses a shiver and sets about making tea. What would we do without tea in a crisis? I let her chatter wash over me. A stout mug is pressed into my cold hands.

'Take a pew.' She shoves over a stool and perches on the swivel chair, hunching into her thin jacket. 'Jings, it'll warm up in a mo. Bet you're feeling the cold after . . . where were you again?'

'Vietnam.'

'Vietnam!' She looks at me like I've just offered her a fancy cocktail, reaches out and tweaks a lock of my hair. 'You've gone so blonde! A regular beach bum. Can girls be beach bums?' Her face changes suddenly, like she's decided it's too early for cocktails. 'We're all here for you, Ellie. If you want to talk about it, come to me. I know what those eejits can be like.'

She glares out of the window. I can make out movement between the car stacks: a bogie piled with car parts being wheeled out; River disappearing into one of the sheds with half an exhaust pipe under his arm. The stacker – the nippy little forklift – whizzes by. Julie's face clears. 'We do have a new recruit though.'

I don't see anyone unfamiliar outside – just my father calling the shots and Offshore Dave lighting an illegal fag behind the toilets. Four days off and he still looks like he's been dipped in a tar pool.

'Don't tell me. He rides a bike.'

'Yes!' Julie's claps like I've just won a grand on a daytime quiz show. 'We call him Rocky and actually . . . Ooh, speak of the devil!' She's spotted something through the window. Her expression goes all coy. She taps at the glass and makes an exaggerated beckoning gesture.

She winks at me, mouthing *Rocky!* as the door opens. I think of all the Rockies I know: the boxer guy; the mountain range; the bull terrier at the post office. The young man who comes through the door resembles none of these. He's about my age, with close-cropped hair, high cheekbones, blue eyes. He's lithe, rather than muscular, sort of light and flexible. I can imagine him toiling uphill with ease on that battered old bike. I bet he takes his feet off the pedals on the downhill run, just for the sheer hell of it. He has that sort of smile.

'I've got printer issues again. Rocky's an IT wizard!' Julie winks at me. 'Rocky, this is the boss's daughter, Ellie.'

The newcomer holds out a hand, and I take it. It's surprisingly clean. 'I am sorry for the trouble you find yourself in.'

His English is very formal, with an accent I can't place. I nod, and he lets go of my hand.

'My name is Piotr, but they call me—'

'Rocky. Yeah, I heard.' I return his smile.

'My name, it means Rock. P-I-O-T-R. But there is a problem with the spelling in Scotland.'

'Piotr.' I try out the spelling in my head, visualise it. It suits him. 'Ignore them. They have to give everyone a nickname. They call my brother Ganges.'

'Ganges?'

'River.'

'Oh.' Piotr nods as if he doesn't really get the connection.

Julie crosses her black silky legs with a sound like a whisper. 'They call me Legs!' she giggles.

Piotr goes a bit red. 'Perhaps I will come back later, to sort you out.'

Julie collapses into giggles and, embarrassingly, I can feel my face start to twitch. I jump in with some comment, tell him to ignore her.

'We can schedule a meeting about it, sweetheart' – she glances at me – 'later.'

Piotr has a wary glint in his eye. He is the sort of guy who will body-swerve a hen party in the pub at all costs, and I warm to him immediately. He says his goodbyes and slinks out of the door. Yes, he's slinky – that describes him. Not in a sly way, but more graceful, like a cat. He's at ease with his body. I shouldn't be noticing, given the circumstances, but I spot Julie raising her gaze from where his arse has just been.

'Cute, eh? Eastern European. Offshore Dave can't stand him "coming over here, stealing our jobs"' – she puts on a very good Dave voice – 'but fuck it, if I wasn't married, I would. He likes the older women, too.'

I can see Piotr nodding to Dave as he crosses the yard. Dave spits on the ground behind him. Older woman? Julie is staring at me again, with a strange expression on her face. It reminds me of the way Sharon Duthie looks when she's digging for information.

'Rocky got on great with your mum.'

I clunk my mug down on the desk. 'What's that supposed to mean?'

'Nothing. Your mum was lovely to everyone. I expect because he's an outsider, they kind of bonded.' Her eyes are all innocence behind spiky lashes.

My chin goes up. '*IS*. My mother *IS* lovely to everyone. I'd better go, in case the police call.'

Julie puts on the sad face again. How am I going to get used to this? How am I ever going to get used to people talking about my mother in the past tense?

At the end of the day, my father stands beside the sink, hands in the air like a surgeon. He nods pointedly to the tap and I do all the things my mother would have done, lifting out the overflowing basin of dirty plates, letting the hot water hammer onto the stainless steel. My mother hates him washing his hands in the kitchen sink. In fairground circles, you never wash in the same place that you eat, but it is my father's house, and he likes to remind her of that.

When Mum moved in with Dad, it was the first time she'd ever lived in a house. Her people, the Smiths, were an old fairground family from Nottingham. You got a job as soon as you were able to count. At the age of seven, little Imelda Smith was taking money for the rides: the swing boats first and then the dodgems. She was a shark with cash, and she was fly enough to squirrel away some 'rainy day dosh' for emergencies. At sixteen, my father came into her life. Already dealing scrap, he was in the market for a vintage steam engine the Smiths had for sale. I don't think he was in the market for a wife, but suddenly Lawler Rook and Imelda Smith were an item, and she was heading north of the border with him.

There's a standing joke around the yard that my dad is the cleanest scrappie on earth. He wears a fresh boiler suit every day, while under the sink there are tins and tins of Swarfega, stockpiled from the cash and carry. Maintaining his cleanliness has become a two-person ritual. My mother spends her life running hot baths and buying the right kind of nail brushes. The dull churn of the washing machine was the soundtrack of my childhood.

He's a difficult man to love. I put it down to the bushy white beard which covers half his face, leaving you with a pale triangle of expression, a thin strip of mouth. His eyes, a startling china blue, are those of a poker player. If babies can read faces before they can make out words, I was screwed from a tender age.

It's become a part of my landscape, the beard, like the pear tree in the front garden, or the car cemetery in the woods. It has its advantages. The other kids thought my dad was the real Santa, and around Christmas time, I would suddenly become the most popular girl at school. It was the best bargaining tool ever. For at least six weeks, I called the shots. I was the Queen of Shore Road Primary, keeping a naughty list of all the kids that pissed me off, like Katie Coutts. I spun a lot of tales. We kept reindeer behind Finella's waterfall and the sleigh was hidden at the back of the yard. That's why we had electronic gates.

My power was only borrowed, unfortunately, and by Hogmanay I was back to being the scrappie's daughter, any gains melting away like frost. My father is a cold, difficult man.

The scalding gush of the water on my fingers gives me an unpleasant jolt. I drop in the plug, watch the sink fill. Dad slips off his watch and his wedding ring and plunges his hands into the sink; applies the nail brush, scrubbing until the skin turns pink. I find myself holding a fresh towel like I've suddenly slipped back to the fifties. The gold band catches my eye. It rolled a little when my father took it off and has come to rest on its side. I can just make out the engraved initials: 'I. S. & L. R.'

My father takes the towel from me to dry his hands, picking up the ring and forcing it over his still-damp knuckle. The look on his face saddens me. I don't think I've ever seen my father cry, not even when Grandma Rook died, although, according to Shelby, she was an old trout and it was time for her to go. My insides start to wobble. I'm not sure how to handle this. I'm quite a tactile person. I do lots of hugging when I'm abroad. I hug hello; I hug goodbye. I rub shoulders; I kiss. I send warm and lovely messages to friends I've only just made, but *here,* at home, I'm stuck to the kitchen floor like it's made of treacle.

Dad looks scared. I catch hold of his hand, pink as a freshly butchered pork chop. We both stare at the wedding ring as if it will magically connect us, both knowing that the only person who can do that is lost. I reach out. His bicep is tough and wiry beneath the soft plaid of his shirt. My eyes are wet, and I'm hot with embarrassment, betraying myself in front of my father. We don't do this. We do oil and diesel. We crush cars. Crushed hearts are a different matter.

My father pets my head. The wedding ring catches in my hair, and I wince a little.

'Good lass,' he says. 'Good lass.' He straps on the watch. 'I've a few calls to make. We'll eat around seven. Just cook whatever you can find. Good girl.'

8

Eight Days After

There are things I should be doing. Unpacking my rucksack, for instance. Hanging up my shorts and sweeping the sand from my bedroom floor. As a teenager, I couldn't wait to get away from here. I didn't just want to fly the nest, I wanted to shoot that nest right out of the tree. I'd had enough of being a Rook. Scraping into university was like winning the lottery. It didn't matter that it was Newcastle, less than a five-hour drive from home; it would be a world away from the grime and the endless walking on eggshells. My mother was delighted. 'It will be the making of you, Ellie Rook,' she'd said. I remember calling her on my first night in halls, sitting in my cell-like room, not knowing a soul.

'Are you lonely?' she wanted to know. 'Are you? I am. I feel so alone.'

She was the one who burst into tears. I was lost for words. How could she be lonely in the family home, with Dad and River and Offshore Dave and Julie and all the rest? I was too naïve to understand. Then, after uni, there was the gap year that kept on going. I graduated from bar work to teaching English, and my visits home became fewer, as I became more settled in my new life. Home had become a dot on the map, someone else's responsibility. Now, the full impact of the situation hits me in the gut, winding me. I feel hollow and scared. Without my mother, this is no longer home.

So I mooch around, letting myself notice all the things I hate about this house. The old-fashioned kitchen that dominates family life hasn't changed much since Grandma Rook's day. The sink unit, the worktops, the appliances are all at random heights, because my mother never complained enough about the inconvenience. The washing machine and the fridge are obsolete brands, because my father picked them up cheap. He keeps a box of vintage parts, in the hope that, one day, something will wear out, and he'll be able to take it to pieces and spread the bits all over the kitchen. I realise now that the only clean, shiny thing in the whole place has always been my mother.

The kitchen table with its mismatched chairs is also a museum piece. It seats the family and all the waifs and strays that come to work in the yard. The men track dirt through the kitchen and strip engine parts on the table, and my mother runs around with newspapers and Mr Muscle, but nobody cares. She is peripheral, like the skirting boards or the wallpaper. Scrap is the beating heart of this home.

I really can't be bothered emptying my rucksack. Sighing, I polish my sunglasses, flick through my passport. I place both items carefully in my knicker drawer. Dirt coloured my childhood; everything was stained by our lifestyle. My underwear is now dazzling white, and I want to keep it that way. I slam the drawer shut.

Flopping down on my bed, I check my phone. I haven't posted anything on Facebook since my father made the awful call that summoned me home. I scroll through all the concerned messages until I reach my final selfie: me drinking sugarcane juice from a coconut shell, on a rare trip to the ocean. I look like a typical backpacker: hair piled up in a bird's nest, grey eyes clear and confident, like I know where I'm going and I don't need a map. Nothing marks the fragility of life like social media.

A name catches my eye. Liam Duthie. We're friends on Facebook, even though I've never had the appetite to reconnect with him in real life. Not since he married Katie Coutts. His comment reads, 'So sorry to hear this, Ellie. I'm back home again for a while. Hope to catch up soon.'

After Paintgate, I became sort-of friends with Katie Coutts. Probably because she was scared of me. We attended each other's birthday parties, but only if mine were held in a public place. Her mother labelled the yard as 'too dangerous', and I was never sure if she was referring to the machinery or us Rooks.

I remember once being invited to Katie's for tea. I didn't really want to go, but my mother said rubbish and buttoned me into a clean white shirt. You need to mix more, she said. Don't be stuck out here like me, with nowhere to go.

Sharon Duthie said Katie's father was one of the 'high heid yins' on the council. I didn't know what that meant, but I couldn't get over how clean he was. He smelled of perfume, not diesel, and he had a round, soft face and even softer hands. My dad had clean hands, but they were a result of much scrubbing. Mr Coutts was naturally clean. When I saw him in the playground, I had to stop myself from sniffing him. The day I was invited for tea, he was waiting for us at the school gate, the only dad in a suit, which was neat and grey. We walked to his car. It was low and black and shiny, and the inside was like marshmallow. I was too shy to speak. I just listened to Mr Coutts questioning Katie about her day and imagined my dad doing that. In my head I practised my replies, even though in real life it would never happen. School was an alien landscape to my father.

The radio pumped piano music round the interior. A scented fir tree danced below the mirror, but the smell of it clashed with Mr Coutts's cologne, and by the time we reached their house I was feeling a bit queasy. I told my dad later about the fir tree, and he said it was criminal. Nothing wrong with the natural smell of a car.

Katie's mother had been smiley and quiet. She'd given us spaghetti bolognese, but I'd never eaten spaghetti before

(Mum never cooked pasta, because Dad hated it) and I'd spilled a bit. As the red sauce seeped into my school shirt like blood, Katie's mother leaped into life and scooped me into the kitchen. She had a library of books on household matters and I had to sit on the counter while she dabbed at me with soda water, vinegar and eventually white spirit. I can remember it so clearly.

'Is it white wine for red stains, Bill? Maybe that's just for red wine, eh, Ellie? Do you know what? Let's just stick it in the wash. The tumble dryer will have it all dry by the time you go home, and your mum won't be any the wiser.'

And then she sees my socks (I'd cast off my school shoes in the hallway, as instructed).

'Oh dear. Let's slip those off too – they're a bit black, aren't they? Have you been tiptoeing through the coal yard?' Laughing, she's unbuttoning my shirt, pulling it off over my head. White cotton fills my mouth, cuts off my protests. I'm sitting there in my grubby vest, sweating with shame, arms crossed so tightly over non-existent breasts that I make a sort-of cleavage. I pray that Mr Coutts will not come in. Mrs Coutts has moved away, stuffing the clothes into the machine, and through the archway I can see my congealing, half-eaten bowl of pasta. Katie is staring at me with disgust. I want to slap her, to tell her this isn't my fault. This is your clean-freak mother. Your marshmallow house.

I'm given a pink top belonging to Katie. It smells funny. We race through the jelly and ice cream, and within the hour I'm dressed again in sparkling white socks and shirt. I smell of alien laundry products. I no longer feel like me, and Katie is refusing to share her toys. I just want to go home, and the pang of longing to be back with my family is so intense I think I might throw up in Mr Coutts's fancy car as it purrs me away.

When I walk into the kitchen, my mother is sitting at the table, reading a book. She must have heard the car door slam as I was deposited in the yard, but maybe she didn't want to speak to Mr Coutts. My mother looks up and sniffs, already scenting outside interference.

'How come you smell of bleach?'

'I had bolognese,' I say wearily.

'Ah.' She goes back to her reading. 'No good can come of foreign food.'

The memory still makes me chuckle a little, although the aftermath was horrible. At school, Katie Coutts told everyone about my grubby vest and socks, and I was tormented endlessly for living on a scrap heap.

As I read Liam's message again, I try to imagine him married to Katie Coutts. My old life is peopled with storybook characters: close the book and they remain the same. But real life isn't like that. Popping across the road to say hello to Liam is bound to open the book at a different chapter. Still, the thought of escaping from the house for a little while is appealing.

I jump off the bed and shove my feet into flip-flops. Woolly socks and sensible shoes are a must if I am going to stay here much longer. The thought is a bottomless well. Slipping the phone into the back pocket of my jeans, I snatch a passing glance in the mirror. My tan is just about managing to hide the worst of the shadows under my eyes. I pat down my mane of hair. Not for Liam's benefit. It just doesn't pay to look too foreign around here. I think of Offshore Dave spitting in Piotr's direction and make a face at my reflection. The girl in the mirror stares back at me with troubled eyes.

I'm about to let myself out the front door when I hear a noise like something being knocked over. The hall is perfectly still; I check all around. My mother is very particular about the hall. The ceiling is painted every year and the rose-patterned carpet is protected by a vinyl runner. Against the staircase, there's an old-fashioned teak telephone table which belonged to Grandma Rook. The Yellow Pages date from 2005. Mum usually has a crystal vase of something fresh posed there: daffodils, maybe, or even just the cuttings from fragrant shrubs. Now the vase is empty.

The noise again. It's coming from the sitting room, as if someone is blundering around in there. An intruder? My heart starts to race, and I press my ear to the white-glossed door. A distinct fluttering sound is coming from within. My hand hovers over the handle, but it takes an angry squawk to make me throw open the door.

Jesus! The crow and I stare at each other for a long moment. I suspect that under those blue-black feathers there's a heart knocking out a rhythm in sync with mine. The bird must have fallen down the chimney – they do that sometimes, when they're quarrelling over roof space. There's soot everywhere, the pristine room stained with the crow's blackness. My mother's favourite owl ornament is lying in pieces on the hearthrug.

The crow tilts its head, all the better to eyeball me with its boot-button eyes. It has something in its beak, but when I take a step forward, it rushes for the window ledge and drops whatever it is. Reluctantly, I pick it up. It's a single green button.

'Get out.' I rush to open the window, gulping in a lungful of fresh air. 'She isn't here. She isn't coming back. Fuck off with your messages.'

I stand back and the crow eyes me for a second. I shoo it up onto the windowsill, and from there it takes its time, fluttering down into the garden as if it does this every day. But this isn't *every day*.

My mother isn't ever coming back.

9

Sharon Duthie is listening intently to my crow story. I rant about the broken ornament and the trail of soot. It's everywhere – on the carpet, the curtains, the walls. She's made coffee, although I'm now in the mood for something stronger.

'You'll need Net White for those curtains. I have a sachet you can have. Just stick it in your wash and Bob's your uncle. Your ma aye fed the birds. Every day. I suppose that was its way of reminding you. Want a KitKat with that, hen?'

She produces a large biscuit tin but I wave it away. I've deliberately not mentioned the button. It is probably nothing more than a coincidence, a green button from someone else's green coat, but I know where Sharon's mind will go. Things are bleak already, without Sharon making them ten times bleaker. I change the subject.

'I like your sweater,' I say. 'Very . . . chunky.' I can't help noticing she's ditched the dressing gown in favour of a handknit and trackie bottoms.

'My sister knit it. I couldn't, not now, not with the arthritis.' She kneads her wrists.

I sense a medical story coming on and quickly head her off. 'Sharon, I was a bit snappy with you, over the newspaper. I'm sorry. All this waiting, it's just—'

'It's bleedin' cruel, that's what it is. The not knowing. That's over a week now.'

Sharon dunks a rich tea biscuit in her cup and devours it before it has a chance to disintegrate. Coffee drips down her multicoloured front. 'I hope you didn't think I was out of turn, lass, speaking about your ma being depressed.'

'No, it's fine.' I pick my words carefully. 'It's hard to tell what people are going through, especially from a distance. People slip through the gaps all the time.'

'I blame Facebook,' says Sharon, with the air of a woman who could change the world, if only folk would listen. 'All those selfies and pictures of food. That's not real. Waking up looking like a troll and cooking beans on toast – *that's* real. Your mum never did Facebook, did she?'

I shake my head. 'She didn't like all the oversharing. The lack of privacy.'

Dad's words, of course. It's Dad that hates Facebook. Mum would probably have quite liked it, left to her own devices. She'd have shared images of ancient trees and cats falling off sofas.

Sharon is giving me her full attention. It's disconcerting. 'She'd stopped using her mobile phone, too. Did you know? Och, you must have known. She blamed the poor—'

'Signal,' I finish for her. 'Rubbish reception round here. I used to email her my photos.'

'Ah. That's nice, lass.'

Sharon is still eyeballing me, but I change the subject. 'So Liam's getting divorced then?'

She's gives a snort. 'Aye, that'll be the day. Not unless Miss High and Mighty helps him pay for it. She works for the council, you know. High up. Got that job through her dad, of course.'

She continues to gossip about the Coutts family. I'm barely listening, staring into the muddy depths of my coffee.

'It costs a fortune, doesn't it?'

'What?' I sit up, realising she's circled back to divorce.

'Divorce costs the earth, doesn't it? I was just chatting to your ma about it only a few weeks ago. I can't believe it.' There's a hitch in her voice. She takes another biscuit. 'Thousands it costs, these days. Bloody solicitors. Your ma seemed to know all about it. She'd done her homework. Oh, listen – there's Liam now. He's been dying to see you. Oh sorry—' She gets all flustered at the word *dying*, but I'm still trying to figure out how to deal with this. Why did my mother suddenly feel the need to overshare, to confide in a gossip like Sharon Duthie? She might as well have tied a red warning flag to the chimney.

Liam hasn't altered much, though his face has filled out in some places and dropped in others. It's as if a slightly disappointed grown-up has been photoshopped onto the boy I once knew. His social media posts show a laughing family man with a wee girl, a wife, cousins. Birthdays, Christmases. Witty comments. The edited highlights. At some point he changed his status to single, but I can't remember being that interested.

In real life, Liam is frayed around the edges and a bit shy. His daughter, Caitlyn, is four, with serious eyes and a mass of tawny ringlets. She's staring at me almost exactly like her mother stared at me when I told the Finella story at Brownies. I decide to go on the attack.

'You know who has a hard stare?'

She shakes her head at me. She's taken root on her father's lap and he's using her to hide behind.

'Paddington. Paddington Bear has a hard stare.' I remember that from my own childhood. I don't know if it will work – I'm crap with kids. Her mouth edges into a smile.

'I like Paddington,' she says. Liam catches my eye and grins. I feel like I've passed a test.

I press on. 'What else do you like?'

She thinks, making a little humming sound. 'Pasta with tomato sauce.'

I bet she never dribbles it on her pristine school clothes. 'Good choice.'

'And my mummy's house. I don't like it here. It smells.'

Liam and I exchange an embarrassed look and the conversation dries up a bit.

'Right.' I get to my feet. 'I have net curtains to wash – and I never thought I'd be saying that.'

Liam struggles out of his chair, Caitlyn clinging to his leg, as if she fears I'll snatch her away. No chance. 'If you need a hand – not with the curtains, with anything – just shout.' Liam's face turns red, and I assure him I will. He rushes on, 'Have they called off the search yet?'

'Um – will they? Call it off?' My stomach grows cold.

'Eventually. Probably after a week or so. They'll downgrade it.' He touches my forearm. I look down at his hand like it's an alien. 'I have a mate, a pilot. I can have a word. They do a lot of voluntary searches and so on. That might . . .'

I wait a beat before answering. 'That would be helpful.'

Liam moves in and gently puts his arms around me. 'You're not alone. Don't ever think that.' I submit to his embrace, unsure of how to extricate myself.

Thankfully, he quickly switches gears. Liam has turned into a great organiser. The boy I knew was always late for class, never managed to get his homework done on time and was always minus his tie or his football boots. But now he makes a quick call to his mate with the plane and plucks an Ordnance Survey map from his mother's magazine rack.

'I'm going to the library to work on my job applications. I'll scan this and we can enlarge it and mark it into sections.'

He swirls his fingers over the bumps and hollows of the east coast. The shoreline is a meandering serpent, and my mother is out there, lost among its coils. I can't bear to think of it, but I can't look away either. Finella's river disgorges onto the beach just a little past this bungalow. It's a hard climb down, or you can go into the village and follow the road to the sea. There's a car park, with the usual tourist benches and bins. A board that highlights the sort of wildlife you'll never see. I find the area on the map.

'I think the police divers have searched the beach here.' My finger hovers over the blue line of the river like a planchette on a Ouija board. It's microscopic, but I can make out 'Den of Finella' in a fine Gothic script.

'There's an outside possibility she may have been swept into a cave. That she's injured but alive. Remember your Finella story?'

I nod. A nerve twitches in my eye. 'The story says Finella may have survived the fall, that she was washed into the sea and picked up by a boat.'

The map shifts abruptly, and Liam's fingers find mine. He shakes my hand a little, as if I'm sleepwalking and he's afraid to wake me.

'You can't do this on your own. Let's set up a Facebook page – ask for volunteers. If we have feet on the ground and an eye in the sky . . .' He doesn't know how to finish that sentence. I nod miserably. The situation is being taken out of my hands. I will drift on in an agony of suspension, or things will start to come to light. Either way, my life is about to come apart.

10

Nine Days After

'Liam's helping me organise a search of the beach.'

It's now Thursday, over a week since Mum disappeared, and we're having elevenses at the kitchen table. It's a morning ritual for Dad – and now River. I'm sure he should be doing schoolwork and not messing about in the scrapyard. I wonder if I should contact his guidance teacher to find out when he's expected back, but they might figure out that it's me who needs guidance.

I've made them strong coffee in their special mugs: 'World's Greatest Boss' for Dad and 'Caution – Mechanic at Work' for River. My mother's favourite *Wallace and Gromit* mug remains on its hook. A plate of Jaffa Cakes occupies the centre of the table, beside the milk jug. The bereavement leaflets that were pinned under there have been binned.

Dad strokes his beard. 'No harm, I suppose. But who'll help us?'

I detect a certain wistfulness in his tone. He is master of his own little universe, and there he can find all the help he needs. His idea of community extends to offering a raffle prize at the village Christmas fair. One year it was a voucher for a free car wash. Our head teacher won it, and I'll never forget her face when she discovered that the 'deluxe vehicle valet' consisted of River and me with a couple of buckets and a bottle of Turtle Wax.

I think of my horrible teatime experience at the Coutts's. I knew that being home again would bring all this stuff back. I expect my father is experiencing that same sense of shame, like the layers of our family are being peeled away to expose the not-very-clean bits.

'The community will rally round.' I look down at my hands. My 'Beach Gold' polish has all but chipped away, and I've started picking at the skin around my nails. I don't know when I started doing that. 'Liam's put up a page on Facebook.'

My father slams down his mug. There's chocolate on his beard, which makes me want to laugh. 'Can no one have a fucking tragedy any more without putting it on Facebook?'

River is glaring at me too.

'He's trying to help. It's what you do, when someone goes missing. He says she might have been swept into a cave . . .'

'Ellie, stop!' My Dad makes a noise like a groan, low in his throat. His hands are balled into fists on either side of his mug. 'Just *stop*. She's not missing. She's drowned.'

River jumps up, goes to his side and hugs him awkwardly. It's then that I realise my father is weeping. I bite at the skin on my fingers until I taste blood.

'You're making it worse! Can't you see that?' River's eyes are black with pain.

'I'm trying to make it better!'

'You're not making it better by pretending she's out there *alive*, stuck in some shitty cave!'

I get up, stiffly. There's a pain inside me that won't let me straighten. River is standing behind my father, hands protectively on his shoulders. We glare at each other across the table.

'We're all hurting, River. But the search – it's all arranged. We're meeting up at Ned's cafe tonight at seven thirty. If you don't want to come, that's up to you.'

'And what will it look like if I don't, eh?'

Suspicious. The word lingers, unspoken, between us.

I phone PC Lorraine Sampson. She answers straight away, and I rush in with my name and my pre-rehearsed speech.

'I don't mean to bother you, but I just wondered if you had my mobile number – in case you wanted to get in touch. With news. If there's any news.'

A pause at the other end – I wonder if she's trying to place me – and then she replies.

'The search is continuing, Ellie. I have your dad's mobile number, and if there are any significant developments, we'll visit you in person.'

Of course they will. Haven't I seen it on all those crime dramas? *We have some bad news for you. Perhaps you'd like to sit down.* But it isn't a crime drama, is it?

'Ellie?'

'Yes. Yes, sorry.'

'Thought we'd been cut off for a minute.'

'Are you treating this as an accident?'

I don't know where that came from. There's another pause.

'Do you have any information that you think might help us, Ellie?'

Lorraine's voice is careful, considered. I feel weird, like a stone has been overturned within me and my insides are creeping with horrible possibilities. I take a shaky breath and hope she doesn't pick up on it.

'No. Nothing.'

'And . . . has your mum ever gone missing before?'

The question catches me off guard. Why is she asking me that? Now the seconds are ticking by and she's waiting for an answer. I bet she's already asked my father, and I bet he said no. She's testing us.

'No.' I hear myself say. 'No. Never.'

'Right. We have to ask.'

'Yes. Absolutely. And I should tell you,' I rush on, 'that my friend is helping me organise a search party. We have a pilot, too, to check out the coast and all that.'

'Yes, that's brilliant,' she says. 'We can certainly get on board with that. We depend very much on voluntary groups in these circumstances because, well, our resources are finite, as I'm sure you understand.'

'Are you going to call off the search?'

'We'll discuss that with you and your family at the appropriate time.'

Brisk. Impersonal. I thank her, say my goodbyes and break the connection. What the hell was I doing, reaching out like that? I've broken the rule. Dad's words rush at me from some dark corner and I feel sick with dread. *We'll keep this between ourselves, as we always do.*

My father returns to the house at 3 p.m. and announces that everyone can knock off early. They've all been a tower of strength, at this difficult time. Let's get some tea on the go, he says, and bacon rolls.

'Bacon rolls for how many?' I didn't sign up for this either. They're all trooping in: Shelby, River, Offshore Dave and Julie. There's no sign of Piotr.

My mother always sticks newspaper on the seats before they sit down, so I grab a copy of the *Gazette* and manage to get a couple of sheets under Offshore Dave's backside before he collapses on the wooden chair, legs spread. His BO is off the scale, masked only slightly by the reek of diesel and tobacco. He leers at me, and I hurry away.

'I'm clean, sweetheart.' Julie sits delicately and crosses her legs. She's wearing a navy gilet and matching pumps. 'Just tea for me. Watching my calories.'

'I'm not sure if I have enough rolls left.'

'You'd better do some shopping.' Dad's face creases up beneath his beard, as if the whole thing is too confusing. I open my mouth to protest, but what's the point. Thankfully, I manage to produce enough bacon rolls for everyone, and Julie helps to make the tea.

She winks at me. 'A woman's work is never done at Rook's Scrappie, eh, hon?'

I feel my face stiffen. Once again, I'm reminded of why I was so desperate to leave: the suffocating *sameness* of every day, and all of us walking on eggshells around my father's odd ways. The day I left for uni, I chucked all I could carry into a rucksack and told my mother to bin the rest. She had wept on that day, too. I didn't come home as often as I said I would, and now sadness seeps through me. Trying to shake it off, I do a quick headcount.

'Wait a minute. There's somebody missing. Where's Piotr?'

'Who?' River takes a huge bite of his roll.

'Rocky.' Julie sips her tea. 'The gorgeous Rocky.'

'Gorgeous, my arse,' says Dave. He wipes his nose on the back of his hand. 'Skulking outside. Probably eats nothing but sauerkraut and pickles.'

'He didn't want to bother you.' River has demolished the remainder of his roll. 'Mum always made us bacon rolls, and Rocky says it's not fair that you should have to do it, with Mum gone.'

'Fuckin' fairy,' says Dave.

I've been kneading a tea towel between my hands. Now I slap it down on the table, ignore my father's disapproval and storm outside. Piotr is sitting on the step of Shelby's caravan. He looks slightly nervous when he sees me marching towards him.

'Don't you eat bacon?'

'I do. I like bacon.'

'Well, get yourself inside. There's a bacon roll for you. It doesn't pay to be too polite around here.' I turn on my heel. He follows me.

There's a moment before we enter when I pause and look at him. He smiles, a little self-consciously. He has a dimple; just the one.

'Thank you.' I say it under my breath, and he dips his head.

After they've gone, I scoop the newspaper from the chairs and sweep mud off the floor. Offshore Dave has left oily finger-marks all over his mug. Sighing, I clear the table and fill the sink with hot water. Before Dad left, he made sure to mention the next meal, just in case I forgot. 'Rustle us up something light, Ellie. Good girl.'

Yanking open the fridge, I crouch down and glare into it. Two eggs, a block of cheese, some wilted spring onions and a jar of curry paste. Worse than *Saturday Kitchen*. What the hell am I going to make with this? The freezer compartment is so frosted it takes me a while to persuade it open. Nothing to see but a half-empty box of fish fingers and an ice-cube tray with no ice. Bloody River – he never refills the ice-cube tray.

I pull out a plastic margarine tub and read the handwritten label on top. Lentil soup. Maybe I could defrost it, and then make rice pudding for afters? The handwriting is my mother's, and my insides catch in pain. I prise the lid from the tub.

It isn't lentil soup.

A large rectangle of something solid is wrapped in frosty cling film. I haul it out and unwind it, mummy-like, from its wrappings, like a child playing pass the parcel. Just as the music is about to stop, I unveil a stack of banknotes.

11

It's River, not Dad, who cuts up rough about the lack of food. I'm still a bit shaken about the freezer find, and I'm not about to share it with anyone, not just yet. I cut him off sharply when he asks what's for tea.

'River, I have no idea. Rake around and find something. You're big enough.'

'I've been working all day.' His voice is a whine that scrapes on my frayed nerves like chalk on slate.

'I don't care! I'm not a fucking skivvy like Mum!'

'Don't fuckin' swear at me.'

River gets up from his seat at the table and looms over me. I see his fists clench and take a step back. When I think of River, I recall a chubby toddler, trailing through the woods after me; a school boy building a rocket out of old plastic bottles on the kitchen table. This isn't my wee brother, this giant with hands like shovels. I'm breathing hard, with fear and injured feelings, and I'm glad when Dad comes in and eases the tension. He jingles some car keys at me.

'Bring back some fish suppers after your meeting.'

He pulls out his wallet and opens it with care, peeling a couple of tenners from the doorstep-sized wad of notes he always carries. He doesn't trust banks. Would he have stowed some dishonest cash in the freezer? It seems unlikely. He doesn't trust us either.

'It's not "my" meeting. We're planning a search party. Aren't you going to come along?'

He shakes his head. 'No, lass. You can tell me how it goes.

Tell them I'm grateful, of course. Maybe I'll come along, to the beach, but I'm not one for crowds.'

'There'll hardly be a crowd.' Does anyone know my mother well enough, care enough about her, to come along? She has no friends apart from Sharon. So much for keeping ourselves to ourselves. 'River?'

My brother just shrugs. He won't meet my eye. 'I'll help look, but I don't want to go to the meeting.'

'Fine.' I grab my phone and purse and storm out.

The car smells like a flower garden. Mum used to place fragrant potpourri in the drinks holder to try to counteract the stink of the yard. A little koala swings gently from the rear-view mirror. She longed to see Australia.

I haven't driven for ages. In Asia, I bombed about the streets on a moped, zipping to and from my job at the Language Centre. I'm still wearing my flip-flops and manage to stall twice before I get out of the yard. I imagine Dad watching me through the window and shaking his head. Maybe River's standing beside him, mimicking his put-downs. They're growing alike.

The village is fifteen minutes down the road, and I've promised to pick up Liam. He's standing at his gate, swinging an empty canvas shopping bag.

'Grabbing some beers for after,' he says, buckling his seatbelt. 'Another thrilling night in front of the box.'

'Could be worse.' Switching off in front of a movie sounds quite appealing. 'I've been ordered to bring back fish suppers. The larder is bare and apparently it's my responsibility.'

He laughs at my tone. 'You've got used to being irresponsible, with all your travelling. Welcome to the real world.'

'The real world isn't necessarily here. I used to think it was, but coming back . . . Jesus, nothing changes. Apart from . . . circumstances.'

Liam sighs. 'Life sucks.'

I want to point out that your wife chucking you out isn't quite the same as your mother falling over a waterfall, but I don't have the energy.

'So what happened, with you and Katie?'

I'm curious. My parents were at the wedding. It was a big affair and my mother couldn't stop talking about the cake and the favours and the bridesmaids' dresses. The guests were given white umbrellas embellished with the couple's initials, although the weather had played fair on the day, with not a drop of rain. Mum's always been great at remembering the tiny details of everything.

'I made a mistake,' Liam says gruffly.

'Another woman?'

'Aye.'

'Ouch.' I make a face like I've been pinched. 'Maybe she'll forgive you in time?'

'It's not looking likely.' He turns to me. 'It's the finances!' I recognise panic when I hear it. 'I can't stay with my mother. I need to get a flat, but I can't afford it, not while I'm signing on. It's hard to get your head round it, ending up back at home.'

'Tell me about it.' I glance in my mirror. Nothing behind me but a clear stretch of road. Ahead, all the old familiar landmarks: Mrs Cheney's storybook cottage; the house that used to be a shop; the low bridge; the sign warning us to slow down for deer.

'You think everything's going to change when you leave home, don't you?' Liam is warming to a theme I don't particularly like. 'The world's your oyster and all that, and then *boom*. You're back where you started.'

'Yeah. Boom,' I echo faintly.

12

The cafe has a large 'CLOSED FOR PRIVATE FUNCTION' sign taped to the door. I suppose it's the nearest Ned, the proprietor, can get to 'SEARCH PARTY HQ'. Although we're a good ten minutes early, a small crowd has already begun to gather inside: anonymous bodies, faces blurred by the condensation on the windows.

We troop in, blinking like owls in the bright yellow light until Ned rescues us. He presses us into a corner booth, from where I'm able to scan the rest of the crowd. I recognise a couple of staff from the Spar and the woman from the post office. Various childhood friends wave at me from across the room. Piotr is here too, sitting alone over a small espresso.

Ned strokes my shoulder. He has a shaved, shiny head and a massive russet beard, gold piercings and a better tan than me. He's a bit camp and writes poems about food which are taped artistically around the kitchen door. My mother loves him. My father not so much.

'Now *what* would you like? It's on the house, sweetie.'

I tell him I'm fine, thanks, and Ned claps his hands a half dozen times and everyone falls silent.

'Okay, people – you know why we're here. I'm not going to say anything, because there is NOTHING we can say that will make this better, but we can DO something, so Liam' – he gives a wide, theatrical gesture – 'is going to give you the low-down.' Ned drops into a spare chair, crosses his legs and takes a sip of what looks like lemon tea. A woman I vaguely recognise leans in and mutters something to him, and Ned makes a reply that sounds like 'We all knew this was on the cards', but I'm too far away to hear properly. I must have imagined it. Liam is on his feet now. I narrow my eyes at Ned, but his expression is unreadable.

Maps are passed around, along with A4 sheets of instructions. Who knew Liam had the capacity to take charge like this?

'Health and safety guidelines,' he says. 'Obviously, nothing will happen until tomorrow morning. If each of you could choose a specific area of beach, we'll note it down.' He brandishes a clipboard. 'We need to look out for any items of interest. Do we know what your mother was wearing, Ellie?'

The question takes me by surprise. All eyes turn to me. 'Um, well, River says she had on a green coat, walking boots and . . . and a red scarf, I think.'

'Where is River?' Ned asks. 'Wouldn't it help if he was here?'

'He . . . wasn't feeling up to it.'

Liam recovers the situation. 'So what we need is for you to be on the lookout not just for . . . for the obvious, but for items of clothing – a belt, a scarf, a shoelace, a button – anything that might belong to Imelda.'

Liam is asking me something, and when I don't react, he reaches for my arm.

'Are you okay, Ellie?'

I need to get out of here. I mumble some excuse, and people shift their knees and chairs to let me clamber past.

The car park at the side is far enough away from the pitying stares. I pace around in the shadows, wishing I was a smoker, that I could take a great jagged breath of something other than cold air and be numbed by it. They do that all the time in films. Real life isn't so accommodating.

The car park is full, although most folk live in the village. Dad used to make us remember people's cars. You never know, he'd say, when you might spot a car and think, ah, that guy owes me money. How many times he lay in wait outside a pub or a shop I don't know – maybe he got Offshore to do it – but by the time I was eight I could identify every make of car on the road.

River was better than me at matching them up with their owners. Dad would test us every time we went out.

Looking round, I realise how out of touch I am. This is now the foreign landscape: grey stone and whipping winds that smell of seaweed and salt. I close my eyes and try to conjure up what I've left behind – warm, spicy breezes and endless sand. Unfinished roads. Unfinished adventures. It's all slipping through my fingers, and I have to face this nightmare.

The cafe door bangs. It's Piotr, not Liam. He comes to stand beside me.

'You are not okay.' His slightly foreign inflection makes it a statement rather than a question.

'No, I'm not. This whole thing . . .' I gesture towards the cafe. 'I didn't expect this. I can't help thinking we should be leaving it to the police.'

Piotr gives a sad smile. 'This from a Rook?'

'You know what I mean. It's too close, too personal. I can't do it.'

'You can do it. You are strong. Anyone who grew up in that place is strong.'

I think he means here, on the east coast, where the gales will flatten you like a blade of grass and the cold seeps into your bones. We are dour and stroppy, but I'm not sure that's the same as being strong.

I pull a doubtful face. 'When the going gets tough, I have a habit of leaving the country.'

'I mean the scrapyard. It is a hard place to live.' He shrugs. 'All that destruction. Shiny metal waiting to be crushed.'

I can find nothing to say. Sometimes people come into your life who make you see things differently. I suspect Piotr is one of those people, but there are things I'm not ready to see.

Piotr inclines his head and says goodnight. 'I will be on the beach tomorrow.'

And off he goes, a tall figure with a backpack, striding down the main street. This is such a one-horse village, I can track him all the way to the narrow lane that leads to the cliffs. I wonder where he lives. As I turn to go back, Liam is standing in the doorway.

'Are you okay?'

'I'm fine.'

'What did he want?'

'Nothing. We were just talking.'

'Bloody Eastern Europeans. I could have had his job. I applied for it.'

'He was a mechanic back in Poland. Have you worked with cars before?'

'No, but that's not the point. British jobs for British workers.'

Suddenly I'm back in high school and Liam is whingeing about not being picked for the football team. I feel suddenly weary. Now all I can think about is bright metal crushed, becoming broken and rusty.

'Oh, give it a rest. Go back inside.'

I give him a push, and we re-enter the cafe.

13

Ten Days After

The landline rings as I'm about to leave the house. I'm lacing up my boots, which haven't had an outing since my sixth-year Duke of Edinburgh hike up Ben Nevis. Clomping into the hall, I stand on the neat rug my mother has positioned beside the telephone table and lift the receiver.

'Hello?'

'Good morning. Is this Mrs Rook?' The voice sounds distracted and far away, as if the caller is multitasking. I can hear my own heartbeat in the handset. *Boom-boom. Boom-boom.* I wasn't expecting my mother's name to pop up like that. Not on the morning I've arranged to look for her body. It's impersonal, out of context, and I don't know how to tell this stranger she's dead. My mother is dead. *She fell from a waterfall – didn't you hear?*

I must have mumbled something, because the caller rushes on, probably juggling coffee and a full diary. Papers shuffle in the distance.

'This is Mandy Cotton from the council's family services unit. I believe you were speaking to my colleague recently, and she's passed on those details to me.'

'Yes?' My heart begins to race. Curiosity kicks in.

'I'd like to arrange a time to come to the house to see you, Mrs Rook, is that all right? We might be better to choose a time when River is actually there.'

There is a short pause. I get the impression Mandy is reading her notes. 'You say that he's refusing school? I can't promise you an instant solution, but if we can start up a dialogue with him . . .'

'Yes, that would be very helpful.' What the hell am I doing?

'Okay. So, from what you were saying to my colleague, his behaviour towards you has been quite aggressive, so let's make it sooner rather than later. We don't want things to escalate. I can do next Monday?'

I make a date, put down the phone. I stand for a long time, waiting for my body to settle, for the cold sweat to dry on my back. I've just misled social services, and my brother is in danger of turning violent?

This nightmare has taken a turn for the worse.

'Bring Ellie over for her tea this evening, son.'

Sharon is pottering about in her overflowing kitchen. She's not going on the search – her ankles wouldn't hold up – but she's coordinating the food, whatever that means. I'm not sure food is even necessary, but I'm being swept along on a tidal wave of compassion and false hope. The Duthies are on a mission, and I can see myself watching from the sidelines.

Sharon is buttering a mountain of bread. She licks her fingers and moves across to the kettle, dog biscuits crunching under her feet. Their Jack Russell stirs in his bed beside the radiator.

'I'll just heat up a pizza, but it'll give you a break from the men. You'll need sturdy boots. Have you got boots, Ellie? Remember it's a shingle beach.'

Shingle is an understatement. The shoreline is filled with whopping great stones, as far as I recall. I don't say anything, just wave towards my ancient walking boots, reclaimed from the cobwebs beneath my bed.

Liam enters with a pile of photocopies, his water bottle, his phone. The maps flutter slightly as Sharon shuffles past him into the hallway. The dog pricks its ears. Things are getting intense. I can hear muttering from the cupboard under the stairs, and then a random string of items emerges from the darkness: an ironing board; a coal scuttle; a tub of rat poison; and finally Sharon, puffing away in reverse like a locomotive, clutching a cool box as big as a small fridge. Liam shakes his head.

I'm already doing a quick headcount: me, Liam, his mother, my father and River – and the cool box – all in the Fiesta. Sharon begins packing it with foil-wrapped sandwiches, two-litre bottles of coke and chocolate biscuits, as if this is nothing more sinister than a family picnic. I'm itching to call the whole thing off, but I have no choice. I have to play my part. I help her secure the lid, listening to her rattling on about her ligaments, and all the while I'm quaking inside.

'It was last November. A wee patch of black ice outside the post office and *boom*. Down I went. Tore all my ligaments – and ligaments are worse than a break. Your life can change in the blink of an eye.'

Boom. I manhandle the cool box towards the front door and the waiting car.

'All it takes is just one slip.'

We bump along the road to the coast, the giant cool box stuffed into the boot, my father riding shotgun with a stout walking stick between his knees, the others squashed into the back. Sharon keeps up a steady stream of chatter which no one responds to. River, squashed between the Duthies on the back seat, spends the whole journey texting. The constant bleeping makes me itch to stop the car and chuck the damn phone out of the window. The radio is blasting out something inappropriate and the DJ is making it worse. *And that was 'Walking on Sunshine' by Katrina and the Waves reminding you to have a great day, folks!*

I switch it off.

When we get to the clifftop car park, people are already parked up. I spot a Land Rover with fluorescent chevrons and 'Mountain Rescue' on the side. People I've never seen before, wearing climbing gear and bobble hats, check their rucksacks and first aid kits. My legs go weak. I'm scared I won't have the energy to search.

Liam slots into his coordinator role, divvying up the squares he's drawn on the map. He confers with mountain rescue, reminds everyone about health and safety. We're just about to move off when Piotr arrives, and again I find myself wondering where he lives. I smile at him.

'Thanks, Piotr. You can come with us.'

Liam glowers at me as we head off down to the beach. There are 355 steps, built into the cliff face by some nineteenth-century philanthropist I can't name. As a child, I counted them more than once. Now here I am, walking in my childish footsteps without my mother. We climb down in single file – Piotr, Liam, me. Simmering resentment stiffens Liam's back, and I wonder how much he'd like to give the foreigner a shove. All it takes is a split second, a lapse. A chill travels up my spine.

I was right about Sharon downplaying the 'shingle'. From where I'm standing, there is no beach, just acres of round tortoiseshell pebbles, sloping to the sea. When we walk, our soles skate over them and our ankles give way. There are mutterings from the searchers. *Treacherous. Watch yourself. Don't want another casualty.*

I strike off on my own, ears filled with the hollow growl of the stones beneath my feet and the mewing of the gulls. The North Sea is different today. I've become used to blue tropical seas, but this one has always been a brute, an elephant seal basking in the mist. Not today, though. Today, the sea rolls over like a porpoise, blue under the shards of sunlight. It has a twinkle in its eye. The ebb of the tide sounds slurred, a lazy *shhh*, broken by the occasional *boom* as a wave hits the waterline. It's saying, 'Look at me. Look at what I can do.' Water obscures things.

My gaze turns to the cliffs, great red lion paws guarding the coast. Between each toe there is an inlet, a chasm, a cave. Liam has been quoting recent cases at me about humans who have survived against the odds: a young surfer plucked alive from the sea after over thirty hours; a diver in the Pentland Firth who drifted away from his boat. But we both know a miracle is unlikely.

As I toil along the shore, assessing the tide marks and the landslips and the serrated rocks, the *boom* and *shhh* of the sea follows me. By the time it gets here, where the Den of Finella spills out onto the beach, the river has dulled to a trickle, broken by its great fall and the profusion of rocks on the shoreline. The rocks are blacker here, sharper, wrapped in chains of seaweed and topped with gulls who watch us keenly.

There are no obvious caves around the mouth of the den, nothing for anyone to cling to. Liam catches up with me and we search in silence, probing all the feasible places with sticks, flattening the coarse marram grass. 'Remember to look for the little things,' Liam says. A belt, a scarf, a shoelace. A button. 'My mother always travelled light,' I reply.

As the morning wears on, the weather turns unseasonably warm. Tempers fray. I pick a fight with Liam over nothing. Lashing my jacket round my waist, I reluctantly retrace my steps and run into Piotr. He produces his finds, spread out on capable hands: a disposable lighter; a scrap of fabric; a hair clip.

I dismiss them all – she didn't smoke, she never tied back her hair – and turn to the sea with a frustrated sigh. The sun is high, light splashing across the surface of the water.

Liam approaches, consulting his phone. 'Okay, so we have approximately two and a half hours before high tide. Is there anywhere else you want to look?'

Glancing around, I see that the search seems to be coming to a natural pause. People are drifting back towards us; the old couple from down the road are sharing a flask of tea. A plane drones overhead and we all look up.

'Paul.' Liam shields his eyes. 'Our guy in the sky.'

Closing my eyes for a brief moment, I imagine being up there, spotting the rabbits scampering on the headland, looking down on the gorse and the tops of the trees. My eyes spring open.

'They say Finella took to the treetops to escape.'

Not surprisingly, no one answers me. Liam takes a swig from his water bottle, and Piotr drops his unappreciated treasure trove onto the pebbles. The hairclip is a child's, with a palm tree and a tiny monkey. I imagine my mother cowering in the branches of a tree. Too afraid to come down. *Shhh*, the sea lulls, and then *boom!* The noise punches me in the chest.

'Jesus Christ!' I dig my fingers into my scalp. 'What's the point? Her body might never be found. It happens all the time.'

Piotr touches my shoulder very gently. 'For today, you have done enough. Maybe tomorrow we try again.'

Liam taps his clipboard. 'All participants will be informed of any future activity. Have you added your email address?'

Piotr gives him a level look. 'I do not own a computer.'

Liam shrugs. 'I expect you'll hear.'

He moves away. I hear him shouting up the beach, rounding up his troops. Calling off the search. The sea is now so bright and blue it makes my eyes smart. Anyone would think I was crying.

14

The trek back up to the car park is steep and exhausting. I just want to get home and collapse on my bed. Draw the curtains, erase the world. Sharon has set up a picnic table in the car park, and River is already there, munching his way through the sandwiches. He avoids my gaze, and I wonder if he's been here the entire time. I never saw him down on the beach. My attention is diverted when Dad climbs onto a bench to deliver a speech. It's unexpected and oddly poignant. He thanks everyone: Liam for the maps, Sharon for the food, mountain rescue for being such a friend to the community. He looks up to the empty sky and thanks Paul, who is probably back at base and nursing a beer. He's grateful for everything. I've never seen my dad like this.

'We're a family that never asks for help,' he says. 'We keep ourselves to ourselves, and when one of us is in trouble, we do our best to get them out of it. The way you've turned out today, to help find my Imelda, my lovely girl—' His voice cracks. The lady from the post office wipes her eyes. 'What you've done here today – I'm proud to think of you as part of our family. You are Rooks, every one of you, and that is the highest praise I can give you.'

The crowd break into spontaneous applause. I stand back a little, taking it all in. One or two individuals appear to dislike being tagged as Rooks, and I can't say I blame them. I've been slagged off for it all my life. The scrappie's daughter. Tinker scum. I've fought it with teeth and nails and brains. The Rook name usually brings out the worst in people – and the worst in me.

But then, as I reflect on his words, I realise how smoothly Dad has brought everyone into *his* fold, on *his* terms. Most people would be glad to count themselves part of a larger community family in times of trouble, but not Dad. Lawler Rook would never give away his power like that.

After the pizza, described by Sharon as 'crispy', but actually rather charred, we drink Liam's beers and watch the news on the small TV in the corner. Sharon shuffles off to the sitting room to watch *The One Show*, leaving us alone in the kitchen. Liam slags off his ex-wife for a while, and I'm just thinking it might be a good time to go home when he suggests taking it upstairs to the bedroom.

'I don't mean like that – no way. It's just that it's become my sitting room. Gets me away from . . .' He nods towards the slightly open door down the hallway. Sharon's cackle competes with the entire audience of *The One Show*. 'And these chairs are hard.'

'Sold.' I get to my feet and take the plates to the sink. When I turn around, Liam is looking very slightly shocked. My face relaxes. 'What? Was that easier than you remember?'

'Oh yes. You were never easy.' He takes a step back and waves me through to the hall.

'Part of my charm!' I wink as I pass him. For a brief second, I am me again.

No, this is not the first time I've been in Liam's bedroom.

Memories of feelings come flooding back: anticipation; dread. Deep kisses, eager fingers, the sound of his mother banging about in the bathroom. Lots of guilt. *We shouldn't be doing this. Someone will hear. My dad will kill me if he finds out.* My sexual awakening was not a happy time. It made me wary, anxious, hiding secrets that never were.

Now, perching on the edge of the bed, I compliment him on the way his duvet matches his curtains. His mother's choice, from Argos. The guitar-wielding rockers have been replaced with safe prints of Johnshaven and Edinburgh Castle. The place smells of fabric conditioner, not the raw teen spirit of Lynx and trainers that used to set my pulse racing.

'What happened to all your posters?'

Liam laughs. 'Rolled up in the wardrobe, along with the rest of the school crap. My mother kept it all. God knows why. It's like travelling back in time every time I hang up my stuff. Remember how we all signed each other's shirts on the last day?'

'Yeah, you signed my boob, as I recall.'

'Did I? I don't remember that.'

'Really? Did you sign everyone's boobs?'

'Probably. I was on a mission back then!'

'Oh, I remember.'

We are conspirators again. His smile melts me, just a little. But this time *my* mother is between us, banging about in my mind. He has a bottle of whisky hidden in the wardrobe, like he did back then, and time slips a little as he pours it into two plastic glasses. I sniff mine and take a prim sip.

'My dad will kill me. You know what?' I flash the glass at him – a clumsy cheers. 'Maybe you only really grow up when you leave home. And when you come back again . . .'

I leave that hanging. He looks around the room, whisky held on his tongue, making that sour lemon face. He nods, swallows.

'And when you come home . . .' He underlines the word with a wave of his tumbler. 'You regress. Have I regressed? Is that how you see me? A loser who's had to return to the fold?'

'Don't put words in my mouth.' I've hit a nerve.

His whisky is disappearing fast as he warms to his grievance. 'You've got the high ground because you *had* to come home. You had no choice. And neither did I, to be honest. I'm stuck here because I can't afford a fuckin' flat. I'm waiting for the council to get back to me, but I . . .'

'Liam, I don't think you're a loser. Where is this coming from?' I dump my glass on the bedside cabinet. My head is starting to ache – with booze, with worry, with lack of sleep. I massage my eyes. 'This is a conversation for another night. I think I'm going to head home.'

He puts aside his own drink and drops down next to me on the bed. We sit, staring gloomily at the carpet.

'Do you remember? In the woods? The first time we . . .' His voice is so soft I can barely make out his words. Too soft, too intense. I remember the Triumph Herald and the mossy smell of rotten upholstery. I remember what happened afterwards, but maybe he doesn't. Maybe he's blocked it out. I hide behind a spark of humour.

'I think about it all the time!'

'You do not.'

'I do.'

'You've been a world away. Bet you never thought about me once. I think about you all the time. I can't get you out of my head.'

I straighten up, blinking at the furniture in front of me, not quite sure how to defuse the situation. 'You got married, had a child. I hope *Katie* never sussed you out!'

'I never felt for Katie what I felt for you.'

'Rubbish!' I snort with laughter. 'We were young. Stupid. It was first love and all that.'

'Is that how you see it?'

I shrug awkwardly. 'I mean . . . of course it was special. Your first time always is. You always remember it.'

'Just cos it was your first time? Not because you thought *I* was special?'

I laugh again, uncertain. I'm not sure what he's getting at. 'You sound like a teenage girl!'

He looks at me like I've stuck him with a pin. 'Thanks.'

'You *were* special. I fancied the pants off you.' I'm still trying to keep it light. 'Those baggy skater jeans with the all the badges!'

'What about now?'

The teenage Liam peers out from this man's face. I catch a glimpse of him, like he's hiding, too shy to come out. 'Now? Now, it's late. It's been a shitty day and I should be getting home.'

I get up. He gets to his feet too. We are synchronised swimmers, struggling for breath and floundering. Our thoughts burst out like air bubbles.

'Liam, thank you so much for organising today.'

'Ellie Rook, I still have feelings for you.'

Bad timing. He reaches for me. I sidestep and put my hands up, like a stop sign.

'Liam Duthie. We're not in school. I've just been searching for my mother on the beach. This is NOT a good time.'

He is immediately contrite. He bangs his forehead. 'You're right. I'm so sorry. I just barged in there, and I don't . . .'

I should have shut him down. Instead, I've left the situation open. He's going to bring this up again when things have settled, resolved. Resolution will be painful. I grab the glass and take a huge gulp which burns all the way down.

'Goodnight, Liam. Thanks so much for all your help.'

He walks me down to the front door, where we embrace awkwardly. Only later, as I get ready for bed, do I take my feelings out and examine them.

15

Liam was the boy all the girls in my class fancied. He was older than me, and by the time I was fifteen, he'd already left school. He didn't go very far – ended up working for a local joiner. In his spare time, he hung about the village with his mates, skateboarding on the pavement and getting in the way of the old folks. Liam wore his hair long and his clothes baggy: skater jeans, red Vans and T-shirts with skulls on. He had a sulky attitude and a bass guitar signed by the lead singer of some obscure indie outfit, which was enough to induct him into any school band in the country.

I fancied him like mad. The Christmas after I turned fifteen, Liam's band were booked to do a fundraiser in the community hall and my friend Rachel got us tickets. She's in New York now, juggling babies and a career in publishing. I occasionally like her posts on Facebook – the ones that don't make me jealous. Anyway, the gig was policed by fathers and older brothers, and the audience comprised about thirty teens trying to look like we knew all the songs. It cost £3 to get in. The band was called Spanner Monkeys. I think one of them worked in the local garage.

They'd perfected about six Blink-182 and Good Charlotte covers, and sang each of them twice. Tipsy on smuggled vodka, we didn't notice. Rachel pushed me to the front. I was a rabbit caught in the spotlights, deafened by the speakers, gazing up at Liam through my fringe. The amps were turned up to the max and the vibration trembled up through the scuffed floor and into my legs. I felt weak and shivery and I knew I'd kiss Liam that night. I knew he'd be my first.

Liam walked me home after that gig. It was a good couple of miles, but it gave us a chance to cool down. I'd scrubbed myself raw in the shower earlier that evening, determined not to carry the stench of the scrappie into town. I was shivering in green combats and a crop top, because my jacket wasn't cool enough for a gig and I'd left it at home. We shared the last bottle of doctored Irn-Bru and walked close together, not quite touching. Liam sang snatches of Blink-182 lyrics, and it seemed that he was singing them to me.

I preferred Avril Lavigne myself, but I hung on to his voice in the dark. Occasionally his guitar case banged off my thigh, and I treasured the feeling.

We reached our respective houses: his on the right, with the blinds all drawn; mine on the left, dark and sleepy, the roof barely visible for trees. The crows were still up, jostling in the pear tree, although they fell silent as we approached.

'They're watching us,' I told him. 'They sense new things.'

'Crap.' He'd laughed at me.

'My mother says so. She feeds the crows. She knows about them.'

'Your mum's a bit freaky.'

'Your mum's always sick.'

We stood in the middle of the road, staring at each other, and it could have ended there. He began to detach himself, I could feel it, but I didn't want the night to end. I slipped my hand into his. Our fingers were warm and sticky with Irn-Bru.

'Will you walk up the drive with me? I'm a bit scared. My mum's seen stuff there.'

His cool, teen-rocker expression slipped a little. 'What stuff?' He followed me slowly, like an unwilling puppy.

'My mother's seen Finella around here,' I whispered.

'What? The chick that jumped the waterfall?'

We'd all grown up with the story. Some of us took it more seriously than others.

'She saw a woman in white, through there . . .' I pointed to the trees that edged the far side of the drive, so thick you couldn't walk through them. 'There's no path in there, but she saw a figure. It disappeared like smoke.'

Being on home turf had given me a surge of power. I knew every scar, each diesel-tainted puddle. My mother always told me that the way to get around a man was to let him think he was in charge. *The more you push, the less you get.* She taught me that. Her whole life was spent trying to get around my father. So I pretended to be scared, and Liam pretended to be brave.

'Do you believe that?' Liam turned wary. His hand wriggled from mine.

'Of course I believe my mother!'

'I believe she *thought* she saw something, but I don't know . . .' He stared at the trees. I saw a nerve tic in his cheek and stifled a giggle.

'I'll protect you!'

I had Liam where I wanted him. In the dark. Alone. Away from Katie Coutts and all the girls who thought I was scrap. But I wasn't sure what to do. Weren't boys supposed to make the first move, or was that just a myth? We'd ended up under the security light beside the big gate into the yard. The halogen glow bleached his face a ghostly white. I was close enough to see the faint red of his pimples and the soft down on his chin. His black hair had a reddish tinge to it. My heart was thumping, and I wondered if he was feeling the same. I press one hand to his black T-shirt, enjoying the pounding of his heart against my palm.

We leaned in until our lips touched; it felt so good, like that first sip of hot chocolate. The warmth channelled down through my belly, and suddenly his arms were around me. The kiss deepened, becoming more frantic, our teeth clashing. I pulled back from the burger-and-booze taste of his tongue. Somewhere, in a parallel universe, I heard the squeak of the yard gate.

A torch beam hit me squarely in the face. Then came my father's voice, unmistakeably angry.

'What's all this? Liam Duthie! Get off my property right now, or you'll be sorry.'

16

Eleven Days After

There are things I need to tackle River about, but it's after 10 a.m. when I finally hear him banging about in the bathroom. As a kid, he was never one for staying in bed, but he's turned into a typical teenager. Eventually, he thumps down the stairs, two at a time, and bursts into the kitchen.

'River, we need to talk.'

'What now? It's Saturday. I've got stuff to do.'

He's on his way out, snatching things up as he goes, like a whirlwind: wallet, phone, a bundle of paperwork. He is shrugging on his jacket, a half-eaten Mars bar clamped in his teeth.

'Wait!' My tone is so sharp that he stops dead, half in, half out of the jacket, chocolate dribbling down his chin. 'Just wait a minute.'

He lowers the Mars bar, wipes his face with the back of his hand. 'What? Has that policewoman called?'

There's a nerve twitching in his jaw. I'm distracted by his darkness. He is a gathering storm, all pent-up energy and near-adult muscle. It takes me a second or two to click.

'Police? Oh, no – no. I expect they're done with us. For now.'

'Shit.' He relaxes visibly and zips up his jacket. 'Your face – I thought something was up.'

'Family services phoned. First thing yesterday.'

His eyebrows shoot up. 'Who?'

'I think it's the paramilitary wing of social services. What have you been up to? Have you been refusing to go to school? Have you been . . .' I grip the edge of the table. 'River, have you been making trouble for Mum?'

'What the fuck are you on about?'

His face turns ugly for a moment. The child River slips further away, and I'm left with a stranger. A pissed-off stranger. He swears some more, a string of words so offensive I find myself wincing. If Mum were here, she'd have chucked him out the house, but she isn't here and now I have to deal with it. I tell him to calm down, which doesn't help.

'Where is this coming from?' he yells. 'I bet it's Mrs fuckin' Cunty.'

'River! You can stop swearing, for a start.'

I've always wondered why someone with a name like Cundy would go into teaching. According to the authorities, she's an inspirational head teacher, and she's about due a long-service medal. But she's never had a high opinion of the Rooks, not since I tried to kill Katie Coutts in first year. 'Violence never solves anything; and cursing might make you feel better, but we need to discuss this in an adult way . . .'

River mutters something about having nothing to say to me, but I have so many things I want to ask him. Was my mother afraid of him? Is this normal teenage behaviour, or is there something deeper going on? The unexplained stash of money in the fridge leaps into my mind. Could my brother have something to do with that? Is he involved in dark dealings – stolen stuff, drugs? There's so much I don't understand, but my brother has already slammed out the door.

An hour later Dad comes in, after an early morning tinkering session in his garage. His hands are cold. I make him a milky coffee and listen to a lecture on his latest renovation project, a vintage Mercedes.

'It'd been left up on blocks in an old stable for two years.'

No antifreeze. I was a bit worried about corrosion in the cylinder heads, but I stripped the engine back and jet-washed the waterways. No fouling of the spark plugs, so that's all good.'

'Dad, I think—'

'Haven't you forgotten something?'

When I look at him blankly, he gestures to his mug. 'My digestives?'

I sigh and reach for the tin. He always has two digestives with his elevenses. 'I'm going out for a walk. I just need to get out, clear my head.'

'Aye, you do that.' He dunks a biscuit in his coffee. 'I'll have some soup for my lunch, about one thirty. There's a good girl.'

I'd thought about trying to share my worries about River with my father, but I know it's pointless. He's never been a hands-on parent, unless you count the back of his hand. As far as he's concerned, kids are women's business. The news that my mother had contacted social services is sure to send him into a rage, and then a massive sulk, so it's easier to say nothing.

Instead of walking, I find myself sitting in my mother's Fiesta, listening to the radio and trying to make sense of it all. The riddle of the money hidden in the freezer is chipping away at me. Chances are there's a rational explanation – or rational for our family, at least – but my gut feeling says otherwise. I can't stop joining the dots, and the picture's pointing to River. My brother has more freedom than I ever had. He goes places with Dad – into bars and other men's garages. Who knows what dodgy contacts he's been making while I've been away?

I sigh heavily as a familiar track riffs into life – Avril Lavigne's 'Sk8er Boi'. I hum along for a bit and catch myself smiling, but the smile fades as quickly as the song. It's a tune from a less complicated time.

A movement in the wing mirror catches my eye. Twisting in my seat, I catch sight of Piotr disappearing into the house, with what looks like a laptop under his arm. His bike, minus the seaweed, is propped up against the back wall. It's a Saturday and the yard is closed. It seems odd, but I no longer know what's normal here. I listen to a few more tracks before deciding fresh air would do me some good.

I used to frequent the woods with Liam. After that first kiss, we had to make sure my dad wasn't about. He was gunning for Liam. *Get off my property!* He couldn't bear me having a mind – or a body – of my own. But I was my father's daughter – resourceful and good at hiding things. My relationship with Liam went underground.

We started meeting in the woods, where we wouldn't be spotted. Dad rarely ventured to the far reaches of his kingdom, so we had the run of the wild places. We wandered for miles, just talking, about things I can't even recall. We sat on fallen logs, leaned up against trees, kissing for what felt like hours, until guilt drove us home.

Only the crows saw me sneaking into the house. I'd slip my boots off in the hall, and Mum would spirit them away. She knew everything, but she never breathed a word. Upstairs, I'd wash away all traces of the outside, change my top, run a brush through my hair. When I crept into the kitchen for supper, Dad would be sorting through a box of dirty, rusty parts on the kitchen table, and he'd look up and tell me I spent far too much time in my bedroom, it wasn't good for me.

The day he found out about what Liam and I got up to in the woods was the worst day of my life.

17

Piotr catches up with me as I pick my way across the patch of wasteland that lies between the yard and the woods. I'm secretly pleased that he's spotted me. There's a feeling of unfinished business between us that I can't quite fathom. I want to know more about him, about how he came to end up in a scrapyard in the wilds of Aberdeenshire.

'I just wondered how you were doing? After the search yesterday?'

I lift my shoulders and let them sag with a sigh. 'I never expected to find anything. It was a waste of time, but Liam wanted to do something. Come with me?'

He falls into step beside me, and we walk on in silence. The grass is like jute matting; it covers all kinds of things that threaten to trip you up or bang your shins. I guide Piotr past the worst of the obstacles – various bits of chain-link, steel tines from something agricultural, a rusty engine, a battery of old tyres. As we weave our way into the woods, I slot into my old landscape as easily as a cog into an engine. A slight sense of ownership makes me even more sure of my step. I can hear him following, the soft shuffle of his work boots in the grass.

My mother once kept a couple of goats here when I was small. Two orphaned kids, one white as a swan, the other piebald, like a traveller's pony. She'd found them tethered in the woods one morning, bleating mournfully. We never found out how they got there, and even though Dad was against them from the start, he allowed her to keep them. One died of natural causes. The other drowned in the pond. We never kept pets after that.

'This is where I come to sort out my head.'

'Your head is not sorted?'

'No. I had a row with my brother this morning.'

'His head is not sorted also.'

It's not a question. We are near the pond, and I come to a halt so abruptly that Piotr nearly crashes into me.

'What do you mean by that? Have . . . have you seen something? Have you seen him lose it?'

'Lose what?'

'His temper! Try and think.' My own voice has gone up a notch.

Piotr shakes his head. 'He is very quiet around your father. Respectful.'

'Because he's scared of him. Have you seen him with my mother?'

Piotr shakes his head, and I swing back to the pond.

'River loved it here, sailing boats, playing at pirates.' I sigh, gazing at the water. It reflects nothing back but broken jigsaw pieces of daylight. The pond has always had a tendency to flood, breaking out in patches throughout the woods like a sky-coloured rash. Trees are reflected in brackish pools; the bits that look solid are not. It's almost like the Everglades. I used to tell River that alligators lurked here, making him deliciously afraid, until he grew too big to be fooled and told me to piss off.

'I've been away too long. I'm not sure I know my brother any more. It's like I see him in my head as this little kid, and now . . . I kind of don't recognise him.'

I pull some seed pods from the nearest twig. They're prickly and hard to shred. I'm aware of how intently Piotr is listening to me, and it's a strange sensation. No one ever listens to me in this place.

'You left him.' The words are so quiet I think I've misheard, but he says it again. 'You left him here.'

His words are a punch in the stomach. 'I didn't *abandon* him. It wasn't like that!'

Piotr is looking at me in a new way, like he knows too much. I'm having a hard time breathing.

'*Shit*. It's so difficult being back. When I went away, my mother said it would be the making of me, but now I feel like I'm being *unmade*, like I'm a stranger and everything's different. Does that make sense? Or maybe it's me that's different.'

Piotr makes a sympathetic face. 'The same is true for me, when I go home. Nothing is as we remember.'

I try to imagine him on his own turf, with his family. His blue eyes have gone as dark as the water. He has a wee scar down low, near his chin. Hidden depths. I realise I'm staring at him and switch my gaze back to the pond. Nothing moves. The steel nose of a shopping trolley pokes upwards like the prow of a sinking boat, and the only thing to break the silence is the creaking call of a bird.

'This place feels a bit . . .' Piotr searches for the right word.

'Forlorn? I always think it feels forlorn.'

I have a sudden unwelcome image of the little goat being fished out of the water by Offshore Dave, it's white fur the colour of rust. Funny how you can block out your worst childhood memories, only for them to bloat and pop up to the surface when you're least expecting it.

His gaze falls away from mine. 'Sometimes you have to leave a place behind to see what's really going on.'

We plough on in silence. Piotr's words really dig themselves in. I *know* what's been going on; I just can't admit it. I had reasons for leaving home, reasons I've never admitted, not even to myself. And now, like River, those home truths have grown up and become unpredictable. I don't want to confront them.

We come to the car cemetery. We always called it that as kids. No one can remember how this drunken line-up of abandoned cars came to be here in the middle of the woods. All I know is that they feature frequently in my nightmares, nestling in the bracken like broken eggs. Soft things ooze from the brittle shells: ribbons of leather, padding, chewed seatbelts, organic and sinuous, knitted with ivy and bramble.

Piotr slows as he catches sight of the long line of abandoned vehicles, but I march on, chanting my way down the line, like a child reciting lessons: Austin, Ford Cortina, Spitfire, Jaguar, Mini, Morris Minor, *that* Triumph Herald. I can't look at the Triumph Herald any more. I think of grit, mouse droppings, chips of glass, leaves. And what happened afterwards.

It's starting to rain: a fine mist. I lift my face up to the sky.

'When I was a teenager, I kissed Liam Duthie on the drive,' I tell Piotr. 'My Dad caught us at it and bellowed, "GET OFF MY PROPERTY!" Like that, at the top of his voice. I always liked to think he was referring to the land. But the truth is, he was talking about me.'

Piotr winces. I can tell he's wondering where I'm going with this.

'He has a garage behind the yard,' I continue.

'I've seen it,' Piotr says quickly, as if he wants to steer me in a more palatable direction. 'He has a Mercedes in there, and an old Morris.'

'A Morris Minor. Oh yes.' I stop for a second. My heart is fluttering like a bird's wing. So delicate. So easily fractured. 'My mother and I – we're his property. Like vintage cars. Lovingly cared for until we step out of line.'

I've said too much. Such thoughts are not for speaking aloud. I'm still staring at the Triumph. I try out a faint laugh. 'If only cars could talk.'

In silent agreement, we turn to go back the way we've come. I imagine the empty eye sockets of the Triumph burning into my back. A sharp pain in my temple threatens to burst into a full-blown headache. The rain has come on a little heavier. Fat drops plop from the trees.

Unexpectedly, Piotr reaches out and touches my arm. It makes me stop and turn, and we stand like that for a moment, his hand warm on my elbow.

'It's difficult,' he says. 'Maybe there will be news. Today. Take a minute. Before you get back.'

He hands me a clean tissue, and I realise I'm weeping. I've probably got week-old mascara all over my cheeks. People say they're beside themselves when they're upset, but this is worse. I am inside myself, looking out. I'm trapped, banging on a windscreen. Screaming, but no one can hear.

Maybe Piotr can hear. He looks like he's seen sorrow before; he has compassion in his eyes. He doesn't speak, doesn't tell me everything will be okay, because, of course, it won't. There's a movement between us, a leaning in. When he opens his arms, I'm there. His embrace is not comforting, like I thought it would be. It's edgy, thrilling. When I raise my face, I'm not sure what to expect. He looks at me for a heartbeat before moving away.

18

Twelve Days After

Liam has sent me a message, asking if I want to have another search of the beach. I don't particularly want to go there with him, but River is skulking in his room and Dad is watching snooker. I fidget with my phone, wondering what to say. I have a vision of him ringing the front doorbell and Dad answering with a face like thunder. Quickly, I type: 'I'll pick you up out the front in ten. Better not come round here.' What am I doing? We're not sixteen any more. I delete the last bit with a small spark of rebellion.

We drive to the coast in near silence, the car radio tuned to some phone-in programme. I let myself get wrapped up for a while in other people's problems. It's easier than dwelling on my own. I pull into the clifftop carpark and cut the engine with a sigh.

There's one other vehicle there – a black Golf with steamy windows and a thumping bass beat. Liam glances at me, but I avoid his gaze. I don't want to go back there. We scramble down the cliff steps. Halfway, there's a bench, dedicated to the Victorian benefactor who built the pathway. We perch on the edge of it, neither of us knowing quite what to do next. The panorama is familiar but always breathtaking: dunes rolling down to the shore and the vast swathe of the sea. There are buildings down there, too: a row of fishermen's bothies, tiny from our bird's-eye perspective. They're all derelict now, long since boarded up by the council.

'We could check the bothies again,' says Liam. I glance at him, wondering if he remembers, but he's looking out to sea. 'Tide's out too. We can do another search of the shoreline.'

I nod, still mapping the place with my eyes. Nothing stirs; even the gulls are muted. The wind is holding its breath. 'The guys searched them last time. I think it was Steve and—'

'There's no harm in looking again.'

'Fine.' I throw up my hands. 'Let's look again.'

He glances at me oddly as I get up. 'It's just a suggestion. I'm only trying to help.'

I force a smile. 'Yes, I know. I'm grateful, honestly.'

'You just don't think there's much hope? Hey, don't give up . . .' He reaches for me but I ignore his hand and carry on stomping down towards the beach.

We check the first bothy. The windows have been kicked out and the door forced in by kids looking for a squat to do drugs and other things. We'd done our share of that years ago, drunk and giggling. I sneak another glance at Liam. The fumbling. Buttons, zips. The deliciousness of it all. The interior always reeked of waste and violence and the dregs of things I don't want to think about now, but back then it was one of the only places we had privacy.

We crush into the doorway, reluctant to enter such a squalid dump. Floorboards have been ripped up for illegal bonfires, and the joists infilled with years of cans and bottles, cardboard, old socks and sleeping bags. It stinks of piss. The only reminder of domesticity is a fireplace at one end and an open staircase at the other, creeping up to a floor that has long since collapsed. There's evidence of it on the ground: skelps of plaster with the wooden slats sticking out like bird bones.

Liam's whole face wrinkles. 'Gross. I can't believe we used to—'

'Don't.' I hold up a hand. So he does remember. 'We were young and desperate. And anyway, it wasn't as bad then.'

84

He sighs, muttering something about still being desperate, but I ignore him and walk on.

The grass is short and very green, close-clipped by rabbits. They've left fairy rings of poo, and a musky smell which is preferable to the one that's stuck in my nose. I take a huge breath of salty air. There are tiny toadstools, like splashes of blood, and the violet flowers Mum used to call self-heal.

Liam catches up with me at the second bothy. I'm hesitating, scenting a change. The chipboard on the left-hand window has been daubed with red paint: 'BLADZ'. And across the door, 'COZ SUCKS DICK', the last word scored out with thick black marker. On the window to the right of the door, the boards have been taken down and plastic fixed to the inside, the sort of heavy-duty clear stuff that is wrapped around new furniture. Someone has left a random collection of objects on the window ledge: a smooth white pebble; half a bird's egg; a razor-clam shell; a twist of leopard-spotted driftwood. Sea glass as blue as the sky. My mother's presence hits me so hard I can hardly breathe. I'm rooted to the spot.

Liam doesn't get any of this. He presses on, shouldering the door. I hear the solid creak of it, and Liam's low whistle.

'What?' Suddenly I'm in on top of him, crowding him. 'What can you see?'

'Someone's living here.'

We step inside. It's a mirror image of the last building, but this place has been cleaned up. It smells of woodsmoke and there is fresh ash in the fire. Clothes on metal hangers are suspended from the staircase: shirts, tees, folded jeans; one of those black suit carriers you see in the backs of company cars. I stare at the mattress, the torch, the water container.

'Jesus.'

We've stumbled into someone else's desperation. The wind shivers through the gaps in the walls. It's a lonely, discordant sound that makes me want to turn round and get the hell out of there.

'Let's just go.'

We back up and Liam softly closes the door. *'Who'd live in a house like this, eh?* Surprised the council aren't on to them.'

I pick up one of the little stones from the window ledge and cup it in my hand, smooth as a peppermint. 'This just reminds me of . . .'

'Just coincidence, that's all. Come on.' Liam jerks his head towards the path. I replace the stone and follow reluctantly.

There are two versions of the night we finally *did it*. The first one is Liam's experience, and in a way, mine too, because I've taken the best bits and put a spin on them. I've concocted a folktale. And then there is the truth. Liam isn't familiar with this version, because the worst bits happened after he'd gone. They're the bits you block out. No amount of spin can ever make them audience-friendly.

We know it's going to happen tonight. Things have altered between us. We have been mooning around like unsatisfied zombies for weeks. He's waiting for me when the school bus pulls up outside my house. We kiss behind the hedge, with tongues. We've been practising a lot and we're getting good: no clashing teeth; just a slow, liquid flow which I can feel all the way down to my toes. 'Tonight,' he breathes when we break apart. 'I'll meet you in the woods.' Then he goes in for his tea, leaving me feeling cold and hopeful and tingly.

'So what are you up to tonight?' Mum says, scraping my half-eaten fry-up into the bin. My insides are too jittery to digest much, and anyway, I don't want to end up stinking of onions.

Dad grunts from behind his copy of *Auto Trader*. 'Don't you have homework?'

Mum jumps to my defence. 'She should be out in the fresh air, these bright nights.'

'Getting up to no good, you mean? Hanging around the village.'

'She's only meeting her friends.'

'Family first. She should be making herself useful round here. You're far too soft.'

I look from one tight face to the other. They've forgotten about me.

'I might go for a walk later,' I say.

Dark comes early under the trees, and we're glad of it, parading up and down the car cemetery, giggling like kids.

'The Cortina?' Liam makes an extravagant gesture, and I shoot him down.

'Piss off! That's an old man's car. Give me a bit of style!'

'The Jag then. We've got to do it in the Jag!' Liam slams a hand on its grey bonnet, and something panics in the undergrowth. A rabbit, probably.

'No seats.' I point out. 'I think we need seats, at least.'

I'm acting all cool and amused, but inside I'm as jittery as the rabbit. I'm worrying about my breath and my body and whether I've shaved my legs properly. I wonder whether it will hurt. Eventually, we choose the Triumph Herald, because it's at the end of the line-up and it still has both doors and a bonnet, with a racy chrome strip in the centre and the letters T and M. The rest have disappeared, along with its wheels. No headlights either, but above the empty sockets the wings are tip-tilted like sarcastic eyebrows.

There's nothing new under the sun, Grandma Rook used to say. Nothing new in the way Liam is prising open the driver's door, bundling me into the back. Nothing new in the way he's snogging me until I can't breathe. 'Slow down,' I say, struggling to sit up. He has two bottles of lemon Hooch and Green Day on his Walkman. We sip and listen, sharing the earphones. Maybe slow isn't the best thing. It gives me time to register my surroundings. The inside of the car smells like a dirty hamster cage, I'm scared to put my hands anywhere but on Liam and the damp is seeping through my jeans. I'd thought about this a lot, but I'd imagined it differently – all soft focus, silky and rose-scented.

Liam is trying to unhook my bra. I sip from the bottle and let him get on with it. Over his shoulder, I catch sight of myself in the rear-view, reduced to one eye and a fragment of hair. I look as if I'm watching myself from a distance.

I've spent months longing for this moment. Liam is here, with his hands inside my top. My breasts seem to swell against him, and I give an experimental moan. We have to put down the bottles. One of them gets kicked over and the Walkman slithers to the floor. Because it seems expected, I unzip his jeans. He's hard and I'm clumsy, so there's a yelp of pain, but it's okay, it's okay, he assures me, terrified I'll stop. I don't stop. His penis is pale in the gloom and I'm curious, but I don't get a chance to explore because things are moving rapidly. Liam is gasping like he's just run up the stairs, and I think it's time I struggled out of my clothes.

It does hurt – a pinching, dragging hurt. I struggle against it for a while, trying to adjust my body to his, but by the time I relax, it's all over. Liam is on top of me, moaning in my ear. We lie for a long time, not speaking, sharing Hooch from the single bottle that survived our flailing legs. The warm wetness on my thighs feels like a badge of honour.

'That was *awesome*,' Liam whispers into my neck. 'We need to do that again.'

I smile in the darkness. I'm not convinced.

19

Thirteen Days After

'River. River!'

I bang so hard on his bedroom door that pain shafts through my knuckles. A muffled F-word from behind the door. I shoulder it open.

'Fuck off! Get out of my room.'

'Come on, River, get up. It's Monday. You need to go back to school.'

The room is gloomy, only the light from the doorway slanting across the carpet. It smells of sweat and kebabs. I make a mental note to get in here after he's gone, scout around for drugs. The dark hump in the bed curls in on itself.

'I'm not going back. Now piss off.'

'We've had this conversation. The woman is coming out to see you today, the one from family services, so you either stay here and speak to her or you go to school. Your choice.'

'Aw, what?' A face appears, a pale blur in the dimness. I want to rip aside the curtains and open a window. 'Why didn't you fucking cancel it? Shit.' He wipes his hands over his face, scratches his head.

I hold the door a little wider. 'Shower. Come on. Shake yourself.'

My mother's words coming out of my mouth. I smile sadly.

I make tea and porridge. Find some bread for toast. River finally rocks up, fully dressed, scrubbing his hair with a towel. He smells clean and damp, like a baby. As a child I loved to hold him, brush his shock of dark hair.

'I'm not going to school.'

'Fine.'

Pick your battles. We sit down on opposite sides of the table and eye each other up.

'I'm sorry for swearing at you. It's the . . . pressure.'

'Is that why you don't want to go to school? Because of Mum? Or is there something else?'

He's tired, vulnerable – ready to talk, perhaps. The toast pops but we don't move. I have him now. Maybe he'll open up, tell me about the money. Tell me what's really going on.

'Like what?'

'River, do you remember when I tried to kill Katie Coutts?'

This catches him off guard, and his face breaks into a slow grin. 'You were the talk of the village for days. A proper legend, you were.'

I wince. 'She had it coming. That girl tormented me all through school.'

'She still has a scar, I've heard.'

It was a Monday when I tried to kill Katie Coutts. I remember because the hurt had been festering all weekend, and by school on Monday I was fit to burst with it. We had netball after school and we were on the same team. As if.

I grab her in the changing room afterwards, pinch her arm.

'I know about you and Liam.'

'What about us?'

'Us? Us? The only fuckin' *us* is Liam and me.' I'm glaring into her face, and she's giving me that blank look, the one she always uses to wiggle out of problems. My fingers bite deeper into her arm, and she twists away.

'Get off me, you tink.'

There's a white mist pooling around my ankles, like I'm standing in a mythical spring and some force is coming up from the earth, pouring into me. Rage is burning in my belly. I want to smash her stupid face in. The mist rises, enveloping me. I hear the sound of my own breathing. My hand connects with her head; the sting ripples through me.

STOP IT!

I hear the words through glass, not connecting them with my actions. My hands are full of her hair. Her eyes, a sludgy seawater grey, are wild and scared. She screams. My fingers are full of hair and it's not connected to anything. I'm looking at it through the white mist.

STOP IT, ELLIE!

The PE teacher pulls me away. A supply teacher, young and out of her depth. Katie Coutts is on the floor, sobbing, and I'm vaguely surprised. I open my fist. A thick chunk of her hair floats down to rest on her leg.

Katie Coutts got off with Liam after a school disco. I'd slept with him six times (I kept a note in my diary, in code, so no one would know; sex was a cheeky little asterisk). Katie Coutts was not going to take that away from me. I'd seen them kissing, but I was so hurt I could do nothing but slink home. Mum had made hot chocolate and asked no questions.

Dad has that white mist. I've seen it. I wonder if my brother has it too.

I come back to the present with a shock.

'The point I'm making is that the rage got to me. I went off on one. I'm pretty easy-going most of the time, but sometimes . . . You know how they talk about a red mist descending? For me, it's like a white mist rising. Like the spray from the waterfall, it soaks me and . . . and in that brief moment, I think I could be capable of *anything*.'

We sit in silence, River mulling this over. He will see himself in me. This will open a door, give us a way into a conversation we need to have. About his pain, his rage. That money in the freezer.

Is he doing drugs because of all the stuff from our childhood? Stuff we've never talked about.

I hold my breath.

River's mouth twists and he gives a little shrug. 'Nah, that's never happened to me.'

I sag in my chair. The moment is lost.

Then he adds, 'You must take after Dad.'

20

The meeting with social services has been cancelled. News of my mother must have filtered through the system, and Mandy Cotton called me this morning. She was sympathetic but stern, hinting that I'd breached data protection guidelines (*Me? You were the one who assumed*) and asking for my father. 'He won't speak to you,' I said. 'Just delete our name from your files.'

I've no idea whether she did or not, because I put the phone down on her. I expect we'll get a sympathetic but stern letter in the post. I didn't let on to my brother that the meeting was cancelled, but he didn't stick around anyway. He put his boots on and disappeared, muttering something about getting breakfast at Ned's.

Sighing, I get up to switch the kettle on and make fresh toast. The ignored slice, now cold, I crumble into pieces for the crows.

With River gone, I sit down to check my emails. There's one from my boss at the Language Centre, Mrs Chang, asking (very gently) when I think I'll be returning – 'We're just wondering what's happening' – and another from Claire, my American flat-mate – 'I'm just wondering what's happening.' I probably owe her rent. It's hard to imagine that two weeks ago I was going about my life: scooting across Hanoi on my moped to teach my English class; sitting on tiny plastic chairs in Chicken Street; downing beers with my friends in the Cafe Pho Co. Just two weeks ago I was paying bills, doing laundry, avoiding cleaning the bathroom.

And now I'm trapped between lives. This one no longer fits, but I can't make the decision to move on. I cannot leave River here to grow into my father.

I should answer my emails, but even that feels like a chore. I sit down with a coffee and scroll through Facebook, but it's painful to see what my friends are up to without me. I turn my mobile face down on the table and let my mind drift.

Liam and me. Our first time. It should spark tender memories. But we didn't know that Dad had followed us that night. What was my father doing, while I was losing my virginity in the back of an abandoned Triumph Herald? Even now, I don't want to think about it. My brain shrivels and curls up at the idea. I suppose that, by not intervening, he gave us enough rope to hang ourselves. What happened next is the stuff of nightmares.

We climbed out of the car, giggling. A bit tipsy, a bit high on life. Clothes were adjusted, buttoned, zipped. Liam tidied my hair behind my ears and told me I was beautiful. I didn't believe that for a minute, of course, but I was elated. A rite of passage had been negotiated, and I'd be able to whisper about it in the right ears at school – and hope it got back to Katie Coutts. She might have the cool parents and the posh home, but I had Liam Duthie.

I was still dusting off flakes of car rust when I spotted my father. His long shadow disentangled itself from the trees, moving forward until he was blocking the path. His white hair glimmered, like water when the light hits it, although I don't think there was much light that night. No romantic full moon for us. Liam swore softly. My heart plummeted.

'Good evening,' my father said. 'I wondered how long it would take. You' – he pointed to Liam – 'what exactly don't you understand about *keep off my property*?'

Liam stuttered something, and I realised my fingers were digging into his arm. I backed off as if I'd been burned. My father's eyes were unreadable pools, but his white brows made a ridge like snow atop a wall. Another shape formed behind him, mean and bulky. Offshore Dave.

'No, Dad, I can explain . . .' My voice had taken on a wheedling tone, the way it did when I wanted to stay up late or borrow cash. Liam was still stuttering excuses, which everyone ignored.

'Dave,' said my father, 'I think this young man needs a cold shower.' And Dave laughed and surged forward to grab Liam by the front of his sweatshirt. He stank of old booze and diesel. He was spoiling for a fight.

It all happened so fast – and so slow at the same time. Offshore Dave bundled a kicking, cursing Liam down to the water's edge. I must have screamed, standing there, rooted to the spot, the white mist rising up through the soles of my feet like steam. And then I was outside of everything, watching myself attack my father, pummelling his chest, yelling abuse at him as the water churned and splashed beside us. Dad stood his ground like a boundary stone, and I only hurt my fists. He waited until I burst into tears, and then he ordered me home. I caught one quick glimpse of Liam's terrified face, water funnelling from his hair, and then, defeated, I went.

The slam of the back door jolts me back to the present.

'What's for lunch, lass?' Dad gazes around expectantly, as if the butler is about to appear with a silver platter.

I shrug, and mutter something about running out of food. Who knew that grieving people could eat so much? Sighing, he peels three twenties from the stash in his wallet.

'Don't forget milk,' he says. 'I'll be looking for my milky coffee at three.'

His words carry me abruptly back to another time, a time I'd been willing myself to forget. I can't bear to think about it now, and anyway, I'm spending far too much time in the past. This isn't the way I roll.

21

I intend to stop at the Spar and buy milk and bread and all the everyday, mundane things that make life go on. Instead, I park up at the cafe, wondering if River is still there. I should speak to him, make things right.

He's sitting at a table, chatting with Ned. I pause for a second, staring through the glass door before I open it, composing a speech. *Look, River, we need to stop arguing. We need to talk.* He's talking now, face grave, a half-eaten croissant clutched in his fingers. Ned's sitting at the table with him. Caring Ned with his liquid eyes.

That's it. Maybe River's gay. That would make him angry, if he couldn't face coming out. My stomach lurches when I think of Dad's reaction. A gay guy in the scrappie? They'd have him for breakfast. Even Piotr gets shit for being foreign.

I open the door slowly, as though trying not to frighten the little birds in the garden. Ned and River glance up, bold crows waiting for me to open my mouth – Ned wearing his concern like a barista's apron, my brother looking slightly confused.

'What are you doing here?' River stuffs the rest of the pastry in his mouth, as if to justify why he's there, but tension lingers around him. I search Ned's face, but it's closed, his expression unreadable.

'Want a coffee, darlin'?'

'No, I just came in to see River.'

Ned rises from the table. 'Be gentle with him.' He looms above us, biceps bulging out of short sleeves, beard freshly oiled and glinting. 'Later, bro.' He touches River on the shoulder before disappearing back into the kitchen.

'I came to see you, *bro,* because we're not finished.' I pull out a chair and sit heavily. 'There's something you're not telling me – although you seem to be able to talk to Ned.'

River swallows the last of his croissant and sips his tea. His face is partially hidden by the chunky white mug, but his eyes are big and watchful. Our mother's eyes, and the way she used to observe, waiting for the right space to speak. Sometimes she never got the right space, not with Dad anyway.

I plough on. 'I want to know about the money, River.'

'What money?'

'The money in the fucking freezer! In the lentil soup tub!' One of the other customers looks up sharply. I lower my voice, leaning closer to my brother. 'What are you hiding, River? Are you into something dodgy? Is that why you're hiding wads of cash? Are you worried about something? Why were you speaking with Ned?'

River rolls his eyes. 'You ask way too many questions, man. I'm not doing drugs, and the money has nothing to do with me. Ned is just a mate. We play poker on Tuesday nights.'

'Poker?' I sit back. I've been away too long. I'm out of my depth. 'Is that where you got the money?'

'No!'

'What about Ned? Are you and Ned . . . River, are you gay?'

River snorts into his tea, and I realise he's laughing. I'm not sure what he finds so amusing – the insinuation or my awkward attempts to connect with him. He grows serious and narrows his eyes at me, the roles suddenly reversed. 'What makes you think that?'

'Because . . .' I dart a glance behind me, but the customers have lost interest in us. They've done the required, *Oh, look at those poor things. Heard about the mother?* and now they've moved on to other topics. 'It's hard, talking about private stuff, especially when you might not be sure of the reaction.'

My brain is already racing ahead. Lawler Rook is more nineteenth century than twenty-first. He's not enlightened. The king would not tolerate a gay prince. There'd be war, and then what would we do? I couldn't leave my brother here, with him. Maybe I could take River travelling with me? We'd hit the road, go to Europe . . .

'You're not even listening.'

'What?' I pull myself back to the present.

'I just said – I was speaking with Ned because he's into all this wacky dream therapy shit and stuff.'

'Dream therapy?'

'Yeah. I've been having these dreams and . . . Fuck.' River drops his mug to the table. 'I don't think I know what's real any more, you know? I have dreams, memories of Mum, but I don't know whether I'm making them up or whether they actually happened.'

My breathing stops for a nanosecond, my chest squeezing shut like a fist. 'Go on. Tell me. What do you think you remember?'

It takes a moment for the words to come out.

'I remember one morning, we were upstairs in my room. I think I was playing with a train or something. Thomas the Tank Engine, probably. You were there.' He looks at me with surprise, as if we've somehow been spirited back. 'I was playing with the train, and you'd been promising to help me build a track in my bedroom. That's right. You'd given me bread and jam.'

I give him a thin smile. I remember that, or at least a version of it.

'Are you going to school, Ellie?'

'It's Sunday, silly.'

'Where's Mamma?'

'Out. She said I was to get your breakfast. What do you want?'

'Bread and strawberry jam. Why is she out so early, Ellie? Where's she gone?'

What he doesn't know was that I'd already been downstairs and had a similar conversation with my father. I'd already rifled through the drawer where Mum kept her purse and keys.

They were still there, and the sight of them made my heart plummet. Something wasn't right. I needed to look for her, but there was my wee brother, oblivious, chattering about Thomas the Tank Engine. I remember how he smelled so clean and wholesome; I wanted to hold him tight and cover his eyes and never let him see anything ugly.

'What then?' I ask him now.

'You brought me bread and jam, but you went away before you could build a track for Thomas. I was up there on my own for ages. I started to get a bit scared. First Mum disappeared, and then you. I didn't know where Dad was. I thought I'd better get dressed, so I put on a Superman outfit. Weird, the things that stick in your head.'

My jaw tenses, but I try to smile. 'It is. It's weird.'

'I went downstairs to see if you were back, and Dad had just come in. He was in a bad mood because he had to wash his hands and Mum wasn't there to dole out the Swarfega. I remember . . .' He takes a deep breath, and his next words come out differently, as if he's once again that scared little boy in the Superman suit. 'Mum came in. She went right past me without speaking. She wasn't walking properly. I looked down, and her feet were all cold and blue, and she only had one shoe on.'

River doesn't know what had happened the night before. He doesn't know about Liam and me, and he probably never will. There are some things that aren't easily discussed between siblings. I'm not sure how much I should tell him now, how much he needs to know.

That night is etched on my brain.

I came running in from the woods and my mother was sitting at the kitchen table, white-faced and tight-lipped. She got up when she saw my tears.

'What happened? What has he done?'

'It's not me, it's Liam. I should have stayed with him.' My voice broke and she clutched me to her, digging her fingers

99

into my jumper. I could feel her heart pounding. 'Offshore Dave was trying to drown him.'

She swore. She'd known I'd been out there in the woods with Liam. I suppose she could guess what we'd been doing. She hugged me tighter. 'It's all right. He won't drown him. He'll be all right.'

'I just ran! I should have stayed.'

'Go on up to bed.' She dropped her arms and gave me a little push.

'No! I want to stay, in case he—'

'Bed.'

Her voice was faint and cold, and I knew better than to argue. There's no point in telling River about how I crept into his bedroom to watch him sleeping, all defenceless, with his arm flung out, as I waited for the slam of the back door. No point in telling him how I breathed in the comfort of his talcum-powder scent as Dad's voice swelled through the house. I couldn't make out what he was saying, just odd combinations of harsh words, filling me with dread. And Mum's wheedling tone, trying to pacify him. Something crashed to the floor and River gasped in his sleep. His relaxed infant fist clenched. I remember the soft blue of his eyelids, the dark shadows in the soft creases of his neck. I'd willed him not to wake up.

My father never hurt me, only the things closest to me.

Fast-forward to the present, and my brother is expectant. He wants me to fill in the gaps, and perhaps it's time. I take a deep breath.

'Okay. I'm going to tell you where Mum was that night. You need to know the truth.'

22

That night, after my father's shouting had stopped, I settled down beside my little brother and let the soft purr of his breathing lull me to sleep. I didn't want to leave him. Maybe I just didn't want to be alone. In the morning, he'd woken me up, bemused but delighted to have company. Was this a new game? I bribed him to stay in bed with *The Gruffalo* and the promise of jam sandwiches, and then I crept downstairs.

My father was alone at the kitchen table, eating a bowl of porridge. My Nokia was lying on the table beside him. It looked oddly vulnerable. Now I knew where he'd got his information from. When I'd pleaded for my own mobile, Mum had been fairly agreeable. It would make me safer, coming home from school in the dark evenings. Dad had been dead against it, until she'd pointed out that he'd be able to get in touch with me at the press of a button. He'd know my whereabouts all the time. At sixteen, I'd thought a wee bit of parental smothering was a small price to pay for the novelty of being able to text Liam Duthie in secret. Except my messages hadn't remained secret. How else would Dad have known what we were planning to get up to in the car cemetery?

He glanced up at me when I demanded to know where my mother was. He replied with a single word.

'Out.'

'Out where?'

He shrugged and continued with his breakfast. 'She walked out. Last night. Your fault.'

Panic bubbled inside me. 'Last night? How is that my fault?'

I rushed to the window. Her car was still in the yard. 'And where's Liam? Did you hurt Liam?'

Dad grunted. 'He went home with a wet arse and a flea in his ear. He's fine. Don't even think about contacting him.'

I raced to grab my phone from the table, but Dad was faster. He scooped it up and hurled it at the wall like a cricket ball. It broke in half and crashed to the floor, bits of it skittering across the tiles.

'You bastard!'

He scraped up the last of his porridge and swallowed as he considered this, before tossing the spoon into the bowl. He wiped his moustache with a square of kitchen roll.

'Your problem, Ellie, is you don't consider other people. You break my rules, and you drag everyone down with you.'

'You mean Mum? She didn't know. She didn't.'

He made a smug *I know better* face and scraped his chair back. 'You'd better clear up these dishes.'

'But Mum—'

He moved to the back door, where his work boots were sitting on a pad of newspaper. 'I can tell you this much,' he said. 'She won't be back today.'

My temples are aching and I feel wrung out, as if I've been crying for days, when in reality I'd remained dry-eyed and calm as I gave River the facts.

I'm in the clifftop car park, my head leaning against the steering wheel. I sit bolt upright as a seagull lands on my bonnet with a thump. Its eyes are round as saucers, and sly. I bang on the windscreen and it takes off with a noisy flapping of wings. It had felt like a momentous moment, sharing all this with my brother. Ned left us alone, waiting until he thought we were finished before approaching us with a fresh pot of coffee.

'I'm not going to give you the whole "tea makes everything

better" crap,' he'd said. 'Coffee won't make it better either, but acknowledging things is sometimes a start.'

I feel drained. Until now, I hadn't realised how little I'd confided in my brother. It feels like we've opened a door, and now the door is stuck. Whether we like it or not, we can't look away from what's out there.

I get out of the car, bundling my jacket around me as the clifftop wind takes away my breath.

I'm not sure what I'm doing here. I should have gone to the Spar, done the shopping and driven home; but I feel the need to be washed clean. I stumble down the steps. The wind is doing its job. The cold is exhilarating.

I couldn't tell River the whole story, of course, because everyone remembers things in their own way. I couldn't tell him precisely what I found that morning. As he said himself, the weirdest things stick in your mind. For me, it's the eerie red gloom of the garage, the dark skeletons of cars. And throwing the milk down the sink. That was my cunning plan. To look for Mum, I not only had to occupy River with bread and jam and the promise of train-track building, but I had to get my father away from the house. Once he'd had his porridge and left, I knew he wouldn't return until his elevenses. By eleven, my mother always had milk heating in a small pot on the stove, and Dad's 'World's Greatest Boss' mug carefully prepared with two and a half spoons of Nescafé. Two digestives on a china plate. But my mother was missing.

At five minutes to eleven, I grabbed the half-full carton of milk and tipped it down the sink. With both taps on full, I didn't hear the door. Only the smell of petrol and old cars told me that Dad was standing behind me. The last telltale dregs of white disappeared down the plughole.

I turned around and held up the empty carton.

He scowled suspiciously. 'You finished the milk? What about my milky coffee? I always have milky coffee at eleven and again at three.'

He started searching for his car keys, and my heart leaped in triumph. I'd have at least thirty minutes until he returned from the shop. After he left, I waited a full two minutes before slipping out the door. Mum couldn't have gone far – no purse, no phone, no car. I knew she wouldn't leave us like that. She wouldn't leave us with him.

Scrambling down the last few steps to the beach, I reach the dunes. I can see the three abandoned bothies, and beyond them, the sea, far out. Unburdening myself to River has brought all my feelings crashing back like waves, and fresh guilt ripples through me as I walk.

I'd thought she might have gone to the woods – climbed a tree, like Finella, to better see the enemy – but I'd left her with the enemy, hadn't I? I'd slept in my brother's room and left her downstairs with him.

That morning, the yard had been like the proverbial Wild West town holed up ready for a gunfight. Blank windows in the Portacabins; the mechanical grabber, that great bird of prey, motionless, its head tilted; and the crows still and silent in the car stacks. I always hated the car stacks – all those squashed bundles of cars, some with their guts exposed, like casualties of war, seats bleeding foam and ripped leather.

There's a man-sized gate in the perimeter fence around the yard, so you can get in without having to unlock the big gate on runners. Dad had left it open a fraction. That was a clue. It seemed unlikely that Mum would have come through the yard, but something made me keep walking.

I found myself heading towards Dad's garage, situated on a little patch of waste ground, within the yard complex but set apart – a bit private, exclusive, like the king's counting house in the nursery rhyme. Maybe he'd locked it, taken the key with him? The door was closed, but with quiet satisfaction I saw that the padlock was hanging loose. Carefully I opened the door.

The interior was dim, lit by the sinister red glow from a battery of heaters he'd salvaged from a derelict office. Hitting the switch didn't help much. The only other light was from a dusty bulb suspended from a beam. Laden shelves occupied one wall, and on the other, rows of spanners hung in size order. Everything was unnaturally neat, arranged, accounted for. And in the centre were his prized cars: a Morris Minor, a vintage Ford and, closest to me, his work in progress, a sports car with its bonnet up. In the eerie gloom, they were silent humps, sleeping beasts. I could smell diesel mixed with stale sweat. It felt hostile: this place didn't want me here. I tried to shake the feeling off. I didn't have much time.

'Mum? Mum?'

The silence was complete. Why would she come in here? She'd be hiding in the woods. I'd misjudged this. But I tried again, louder.

'Mum?'

The word sat heavy in the air. I heard a tapping. Faint at first, but growing stronger. A muffled voice: 'Ellie? Ellie!'

It was coming from the boot of the Morris Minor.

'Mum? What the hell?' I was over in a flash, rattling the handle.

Mum's voice, faint and measured: 'It's okay, sweetheart. I'm okay.'

'It's locked, Mum. What do I do?'

My chest grew tight with fear, my hands slippery with panic.

'Get the key.' Her voice sounded rusty. 'It's hanging up somewhere.' A tight band of anxiety wrapped around my head. I ran to the tool racks, scouted high and low, disturbing spanners and screwdrivers and musty rags. A hammer crashed to the concrete, narrowly missing my foot. Where would my father leave a bunch of keys? Where would he hide them?

An old kitchen cabinet sat in the corner beside his workbench – one of those old-fashioned ones with the frosted glass doors at the top and the drop-down front. Once, it must have held Grandma Rook's china, but now it was groaning with grease guns and cans of spray paint. There were three drawers, and I hauled out the top one – a litter of nuts, bolts and metal brackets nesting on yellow newspaper. There was a metal box, the kind you keep cash in. Frantically, I pulled it out, breaking a nail as I set about prising it open. Mum's silence spurred me on more than her words. The key was still in the lock. With a sudden twist I was confronted with a mad tangle of discarded keys. Elation turned to anger. How the hell was I supposed to figure out which key?

'I found a box of bloody keys, Mum, but I don't know—'

'The Morris key fob – look for that. A bull on it.'

'I've got it!' It was sitting on the top of the pile, a blue and white badge with a red bull pinned to a scuffed leather fob. It took me a few minutes to insert the key, my hand was shaking so badly. Mum had gone silent again, but as soon as the lock clicked, the boot sprang open with a groan. A waft of that old-carpet smell took me right back to the woods, to what I'd done with Liam to cause this. *You must have known.* Dad's voice swelling up through the ceiling. *I'll teach you . . . fucking covering up for her.*

I didn't have time to dwell on it. My mother was curled up, a crumpled doll in a toybox. An elbow, a denim-clad knee, one bare foot. In the red light, her toes looked purple with cold.

'Jesus, Mum!' I grabbed at her arms, her legs, pulling her into a Mum-shape, straightening her up. She groaned, just like the boot lid. I searched the space around the spare wheel for her other shoe but could find nothing.

Mum swallowed once, painfully, and licked dry lips. 'Somewhere out there.'

I wasn't certain whether she was referring to the lost shoe or my father. I could think of nothing comforting to say, so I just gave her a hug. She was unresponsive, staring straight ahead, her pupils contracting in the strange red light.

'He's gone for milk,' I whispered. She reached for my hand and squeezed it. Maybe I could smuggle her in before he came back.

Back in the present, I play the scenes over and over in my head. I've reached the sea without noticing, and it's a shock to find myself here on the shoreline. The tide is out. Halfway to the horizon, a fishing boat, red against the blue, chugs into open water, trailing a white cloud of squabbling herring gulls.

Mum used to take River and me to the beach as often as she could. She encouraged us to tell stories about the alien landscape revealed at low tide: sandy deserts; slimy green mountain ranges; bottomless black pools. A magical place, far away from the scrapyard.

But, at some point, you have to get real.

My father was at the sink when I helped my mother back into the house. River was right – she was crushed and broken, like a doll. Dad didn't notice at first, too busy wiping down the fresh milk cartons before storing them in the fridge. River, now dressed in his Superman outfit, was at the table, pulling the limbs off some plastic figures. Mum walked right past them. She was holding herself all funny, like it hurt to be properly upright, and limping a little, on account of the single shoe. I think she was making for the bathroom – she must have been desperate for a pee after being shut up like that all night. She walked right past them. Even when River shouted, 'I missed you, Mamma,' and Dad muttered, 'I'm sorry, darlin',' under his breath, she kept right on going.

23

A crow hops into my line of vision, far out, on the exposed sandbar. He's on a mission, pausing now and then with his head cocked. He picks up a sprig of seaweed, discards it. Walks on. He's spotted something, he's gathering speed, and the big white terrors descend from the sky with their weeping and wailing. It's something dark; I can see it from here. A piece of rubbish – cloth, perhaps – buried in the sand.

The crow stops, eyeballs his prize. He investigates it with the tip of his beak, gives it a test pull. There's a bit of give in it, and the crow really starts to go for it, determined, unearthing a ribbon of dark matter from the sand.

I imagine what Liam would do, if he were here. He'd be racing down there with his clipboard. *Remember, we need to look for the little things*, he'd be saying. A belt, a scarf, a shoelace. A button. The clues are all there. My heart twists. I edge closer. The ground alters under my feet as I venture from the dry sand. Below the tideline, the rock pools are deep and the seaweed is like bright green jelly beneath my boots. I slip more than once. One slip is all it takes. *Boom.*

The crow flaps upwards and settles some distance away. He watches as I pick my way over the rocks, waiting to see what I'll do next. Will I go for his treasure, his telltale, tip-of-the-iceberg fold of fabric? His head tilts to one side. I reckon he's laughing at me. And just like that, my heel skids on the slimy green. I land heavily on my backside in one of the pools. Embarrassed and floundering, I regain my feet, but the bird has flown, and whatever desire I had to investigate further goes with it.

What the hell am I doing? My clothes are as heavy as my spirits as I turn around and drag myself back to the beach.

I realise belatedly that someone apart from the crow has witnessed my pratfall. A lone figure, watching from the shore. I struggle up to him.

Piotr's face is solemn. 'Did you see something, Ellie? Did you find anything?'

I look at him blankly for a second. 'What? Oh, no. Low tide, eh? Lots of . . . stuff. I saw a crow pulling at something and I thought . . . Phew, I'm thinking too much. I need a break from thinking.'

We both glance down at my legs. My jeans are black with water; it's funnelling down the crack in my backside. It's bloody freezing. Piotr is no doubt mistaking my pained expression for extreme anguish. He springs into old-fashioned-gentleman mode.

'Here, let me help you. You're soaked.'

'Just a bit.' I smile, but I avoid his helping hand and march ahead of him up to the stony beach. My feet are slopping around in my boots, my jeans are plastered to my skin and the hem of my jacket is saturated. And I have to drive home like this.

'Come home with me. I will give you a towel,' Piotr says, as if he can read my mind.

It's a tempting offer. My teeth are beginning to chatter.

'Um, okay. But . . .' I'm about to ask where he lives when he makes a sweeping gesture towards the fishing bothies, and everything clicks into place. We head towards the second bothy, the place that had given me a glimpse into someone else's desperation.

'Did you see me and Liam, that time? Having a nosy?'

He nods. 'I was up on the cliff. You guessed who lived here?'

'No. No, I never thought of you.' I feel a bit awkward now, like I've been rumbled snooping through his stuff. 'It's okay. I won't tell anyone. I'm a Rook – we don't like people knowing our business either.'

His face softens at that, and I recognise a little chink of myself. He busies himself with the door, which seems to be unlocked but firmly wedged shut.

'No one cares who lives here.' He addresses the wooden planks as he puts his shoulder to them. 'If not me, the junkies will use it.'

My gaze drops to the window ledge, the beachcomber's collection I'd noticed before: sea glass, pebbles, tiny shells. The door gives way with a loud creak and Piotr holds it open for us both to enter, me shuffling along like an old lady in my cold, clinging clothes. Piotr's warm hand touches my back.

'You are freezing to death!'

'N-not quite.' I'm so cold I actually feel sick. I slip off my coat, and he shakes it out and hooks it over the back of a pine chair beside the hearth. A fire is blazing in the grate, but it feels like a sham, a garden bonfire that might burn out at any moment, leaving us in the dark. Woodsmoke and fresh pine logs cover up other, less savoury smells: damp; mice. I pluck miserably at my soaking jeans and he goes on the hunt for a towel, returning to hand me a huge bath sheet printed with palm trees and parrots. It takes me back to Asia on a wave of nostalgia. I was sunbathing on a towel like that just two weeks ago, but it's all receding, like a dream, and I can't bear it. Piotr mistakes my stupor and takes the towel from me to drape it gently round my shoulders.

'I go outside. Let you be private.'

He slips out, closing the door tactfully behind him. The Asian dream snuffs out, and I'm presented with the novelty of stripping off in an abandoned building, in close proximity to a man I know nothing about.

My gaze travels over the walls. The plasterwork is holding up in places, but where it's given up the fight, exposed spars of wood jut out like splintered bone. In one corner is the staircase I noticed before, clothes neatly suspended from it, and beneath it, a makeshift bed. A blue plastic lemonade crate, faded by the sea, serves as a bedside table. I can see a paperback and some reading glasses. A bottle of water. There are cardboard boxes stacked against the far wall. *Del Monte Peaches. Bananas.*

If I'm going to take my wet clothes off before Piotr, a virtual stranger, returns to this derelict squat, I'd better get on with it. I peel off my jeans and knickers and arrange them carefully over the piled-up logs in the hearth. I spot a single heavy-duty glove perched on top of a half-bucket of coal. A red right-hand glove. It reminds me of that Nick Cave song, the one about the shady character who's pulling everyone's strings. My father will be baying for milk for his coffee right about now. If he could see me here.

The towel is thin and flat from frequent washings, but it smells fresh and it does the job, rubbing life into my raw, stinging skin. Keeping my top on, I tie the towel around my waist like a sarong.

Settling on the chair, I stretch my toes out towards the blaze. I'm beginning to thaw. My stomach unclenches. It's a welcome relief to sit here, swaddled in an oversize towel, lulled by the steady crackle of the flames. There's an open laptop balanced on a wooden box nearby, and my mind drifts to the weekend, and Piotr's strange visit to my father, laptop under his arm. Why is he at home today? The door creaks behind me and I swing my head round.

'Why aren't you in the yard?' I sound more accusatory than I mean to be. I guess the warmth of the fire hasn't thawed me out completely.

'Your father has given me the day off to do some bookwork for him.' He nods towards the laptop. 'I will continue until the battery runs out, and then I will go to the cafe to recharge.'

No electricity or water. I wonder how he can bear to live like this, and then I think of Shelby and his creed of 'just passing through' – while enjoying all the meals and free electricity he can consume. Or me, a gap year adventurer turned wage slave, albeit slaving in the sun. Maybe Piotr has it sussed. My curiosity is growing into fascination. 'What kind of bookwork do you do for my father? Dodgy dealings, no doubt, or he'd get Julie to do it.'

Piotr's smile has a mischievous slant. 'Rooks don't like people knowing their business.'

That makes me giggle. 'You've been here too long, Piotr. You need to leave before you get sucked in. Look at Shelby; he only came for a few weeks.'

The thought makes me sad again. I feel like Shelby has been thwarted in his life, but I'm not exactly sure why.

Piotr crosses to the corner near the front window, which is sheeted with plastic. I can see a table, a plastic washing-up bowl and a tray of kitchen utensils. He returns with a tumbler of what looks like water. I'd been hoping for a cup of tea, but I accept it gratefully and take a sip. My sudden coughing fit makes him smile.

'For shock.'

I grasp my throat. 'Jesus, that's got a kick.' A different kind of heat sizzles all the way down to my belly. 'Isn't it a bit early for this? I should be getting home. I only came out to get milk.'

Piotr overturns one of the bigger logs stacked by the hearth and, using it as a makeshift stool, sinks down onto it. I'm suddenly aware of how close we are. He raises his glass, which sparkles in the firelight.

'Polish vodka – it will chase away the cold. And it's three o'clock.'

'Shit.' A picture of my father waiting impatiently for his milky coffee makes me take a bigger gulp of the vodka than I should, but any desire to rush home seems to be fading. 'Oh well – I guess it's five o'clock somewhere!'

I smile, and the vodka slops unpredictably around my glass when I raise it to him.

24

'Here's to you, Piotr the Rock.'

We clink glasses as if we've just met in a bar.

'To you, Ellie the Rook.'

We exchange a conspiratorial grin. He's the sort of man I'd like to clink glasses with in a bar. He'd be on business, perhaps, dressed in a smart suit, and I'd be wearing a strappy sundress and make-up. My face would be alive with mischief, not tight with anxiety, and we'd flirt with each other and exchange clever banter. We'd leave reality at the door. Whatever happened between us would be simple and sweet and life-affirming. I swallow some more vodka, feel the buzz. I'm halfway there already.

As we smile into each other's eyes, my tropical towel slips, revealing a little too much leg. I don't rush to cover up, happy to watch Piotr's gaze slide to my thigh. Warmth stirs deep inside me. I need his warmth right now. I'm acutely aware of our aloneness, our proximity, my knickers draped across his woodpile.

'If I close my eyes,' I whisper, 'I can imagine I'm at the beach, a long, long way from here. Heat and sand and strong liquor, and nothing to worry about but me.'

Polish vodka is good stuff. My eyes flutter shut. I'm aware of the rosy red glow of the fire on the backs of my eyelids. I hear him move, and his shadow flits across my inner vision. I can smell the woodsmoke on his jumper, and when his lips touch mine I realise that this is what I've been waiting for. I savour the vodka taste of his tongue. This should not be happening, but I don't try to stop it. To move might be to break the tenuous thread that connects us. I don't want the outside world to intrude; all that common sense. This is just for me. The taste of Piotr's mouth, the dripping-honey heat inside.

This is insane. Do I say that aloud when we break apart for breath? I can't be sure. His eyes are like the fire. I can see pictures in them: things I don't know; things I want to find out. He's been kneeling on the floor beside me, but now he gets up, pulling me with him. A glass gets knocked over and vodka pools beneath my toes. The towel slips. His clothes feel rough and exciting against my bare skin; his hands travel over my hips. I search for his mouth again and everything melts away.

We have to break apart briefly as he strips off his jumper. I help, unwilling to separate from him. He peels off my T-shirt, unhooks my bra. I wonder how many times he's done this with strange women in this dilapidated place. My cautious self hesitates. The path is unknown and dangerous. One slip is all it takes, and *boom*. But I want to be swept away by his vitality, to be caught up in some raw emotion that has nothing to do with loss and hurt. If I have to fall, it may as well be here, with him.

We make it to the bed in the corner. It's piled with a couple of duvets and a blue nylon sleeping bag. His weight presses me down onto the thin mattress, and I can feel the lumps and bumps of the floor, jagged edges of stone. I make some lame joke about being between Rocky and a hard place, which he doesn't get, but it doesn't matter. It's not real. It's a fairy tale, probably one that ends with a dark moral. The scrap princess and the pea.

Piotr is kissing my neck and I don't want him to stop, but he pauses, drawing back to cup my face. When he looks down into my eyes, I see curiosity, an invitation. Intimacy is dangerous. I don't want that. I turn my head, examine the crude whitewashed wall. My hand sneaks down between us to take hold of him, play with his hardness, his need. He groans and I smile at the crumbling plaster. There is no going back.

I jerk awake to find myself curled up against Piotr like a baby. Our skin is damp where we've been pressed together. My right arm is locked around his back, trapped by his sleeping weight. I draw away carefully, and he stirs a little, but his eyes remain closed. Sleep makes you vulnerable. That's what I'm afraid of. When you sleep, you're not in control.

Time to make a tactical withdrawal. That other girl, the one who sips cocktails on foreign beaches, she doesn't make a habit of one-night stands. That stranger-in-the-bar scenario has only happened twice, and I'm not sure of the protocol. I've brought a fragment of my new life into my old one and I'm not sure how it fits. It can't fit. I see my father's face again and struggle into a sitting position. Cold air pinches my nose. The fire has died down, and without its rosy glow the place looks stained and broken. Something skitters behind one of the piled-up boxes. I feel cold inside.

Piotr's eyes flick open. He reaches for me but I shuffle away, get to my feet. Despite our intimacy, it feels odd being naked in front of him. I suddenly feel the need to be fully dressed and in control. I dress from the top down – bra, T-shirt. My knickers are dry but my jeans are still damp to the touch. I wriggle into them. Only then do I turn to face him. He's lying on his side, resting on one elbow, watching me, but not with lust. It's hard to read his expression.

'Don't just go like this,' he says. 'We need to talk.'

I come over to the bed, gaze down at him. *We need to talk.* Isn't that what people say when they're trying to pin you down? Perhaps I shouldn't have complicated this with sex. I didn't set out to, but sometimes life just *is* complicated. I don't know how I can possibly fit Piotr into this mess, and yet . . . And yet I want to try. I'm not ready to let him go.

'There's something I have to tell you,' he says softly. 'I should have told you before.'

I sit back down on the edge of the mattress. He holds out his hand and I take it. It's warm and strong and I clasp it tighter than I feel I should.

'It's about your mother.'

25

As I exit Piotr's dwelling, I pause to survey my mother's odd little collection of beach finds on the window ledge, picking up the bone-like stem of a clay pipe and turning it over in my fingers, just as I'm now turning Piotr's revelations over in my head. Everything he just told me is wrong on so many levels. It's not what I expected, but somehow, it's worse. My mother's lies, my father's schemes – secrets on top of secrets. There are gaps in Piotr's version of the truth, of course, but I think I'm starting to piece it all together. White mist seems to steam from my damp clothes. A tight little pocket of anger is threatening to burst in my throat. I want to scream into the never-ending wind in this godforsaken place. In a single sweep I scrape up the glass, the pebbles, the shells and stuff a handful of them into my jacket pocket, before striding away across the sand. I think I hear Piotr call after me, but I'm so furious I don't look back.

My drive home is a blur. I have the presence of mind to stop for milk, but after that, all I'm aware of is my fists clenched on the steering wheel, tears welling in my eyes. When my vision became dangerously blurry, I brake at the side of the road and let myself weep. It all came out in a strangled, choked-up storm of emotion. What is that saying of Shelby's? *Hold the line*. I have to keep my nerve. I'm weeping not just for my mother, but for myself; for the way the scrappie has always cast a long, dirty shadow over everything I do. In another life, Piotr could have meant something to me. If we'd met far away from here . . . But whatever we might have had is now polluted with distrust and secrets and the spectre of my father pulling our strings.

In a fit of temper, I scoop my mother's shells and stones and sea glass from my pocket and pelt them across the car. They hit the dashboard and scatter in an explosion of green and blue and bone white.

Oh, Mum. The words are wrung from my soul. I realise I'm furious with my mother. *What have you done?* She has deserted us. Abandoned us in a place I don't know any more.

With a man I don't trust.

Back in the yard, I clamber from the driver's seat. I'm not ready to face my father yet. I want to speak to Shelby, but his Land Rover is missing and the caravan is locked up with a chain and padlock. At some point the Yale has been broken, and an old-fashioned hasp has been welded to the door. The caravan reminds me of a big tin toolbox – the nuts and bolts of Shelby's life neatly stored in one place. I've always envied Shelby, that he can put down his wheels here and be content never to stray from the yard. Maybe what I have to tell him will jerk him out of his complacency. I need to find out how much he really knows about what's been going on here.

Where is Shel when I need him? I shake the chain, as if that will magically conjure him from the ether. My life is suddenly, inexplicably, full of other people's secrets, and I'm not sure how much more I can take. As a family, we've been quiet for too long. Complicit.

Turning away from the caravan, I spot River at the back door, scraping mud from his boots with a screwdriver. When he looks up, his cheeks are flushed, like he's been putting all his energy into the task.

'You're in trouble,' he mutters.

I hold up a plastic carton of milk. 'Did he miss his elevenses? What a fuckin' shame.'

My brother raises his eyebrows in disbelief. 'Seriously. He had to have Irn-Bru.'

He shakes his head and goes back to his task.

My father is checking his iPhone at the kitchen table. It's the latest model, acquired for him by Offshore Dave through an under-the-table transaction in an Aberdeen bar. There's a can of Irn-Bru to his left and the biscuit tin is open, but I know he won't have had one. He can only eat digestives with coffee, and he can only drink his coffee with milk. He doesn't look in my direction, and the silence stretches between us as I place the milk carefully on the table and shrug off my jacket. The white mist has dissipated, leaving an overwhelming need to apologise. In this moment I hate myself.

'You're sorry? You're over' – he consults his watch, despite holding all that technology in his hand – 'two hours late. Two hours. Did you have car trouble?'

His blue eyes are blasting through me, as if he can see the livid beat of my heart. I don't say anything, just make myself busy, wiping down the milk carton before placing it in the fridge, handle facing to the left, in the approved way.

'You've been parked up at the beach.'

'I was upset. I thought I'd go down there and take a few minutes, but I ended up searching. Just in case.'

'That was your mother's line: "I'm just going to the beach." I didn't believe her, and I don't believe you. I know who lives at the beach.'

My father pushes back his chair. Still dodging his gaze, I set about cleaning the sink.

'You were with Rocky.'

It isn't a question. Life rewinds like a runaway film reel. Liam, Mum, humiliation, horror. I'm a kid again, flushed and frightened, wanting to dissolve through the cracks in the floor. I hear the scrape of his chair on the tiles, the measured tread of his steps behind me. He's never in a hurry, Dad. He knows he'll get his own way without trying, a lazy lion contemplating a gazelle. Adrenaline floods my system, but instead of either fight or flight, I choose the path of least resistance. I get stuck into the porridge pot with a wire scouring pad. 'I met him on the beach. He helped me to search.'

My father's hand comes into contact with my left buttock. He squeezes it, like he's measuring up a side of pork. I squirm away from him.

'Your jeans are wet.'

'I tripped. I fell in a rockpool.'

'Your top—'

I toss the scouring pad into the sink and pick up a butter knife from the draining board, using it to chip away at the stubborn goo on the bottom of the pan. 'No, my top was okay. It was just my jeans and my boots.' I can scarcely breathe. Mum is no longer here to come between us and I don't know what he'll do.

'Your top.' His voice is very close to my ear. I can almost feel him breathing on me. I pause in my scraping. How much damage could I do with a butter knife? I imagine pinning his hand to the counter like a dead butterfly. 'Your top is inside out.'

My breathing stops altogether. He flicks the offending label and then grabs a handful of fabric. With a jerk, the neckline tightens around my throat like cheese wire. My objections turn into a choking cough. He shakes me like a disobedient puppy.

'You stay away from fuckin' Rocky, do you hear? He's on his last warning. I've been through all this with your mother.'

His grip loosens, but he slaps me so hard across the back of the head that my teeth rattle. Pain blooms through my sinuses and the water in the sink erupts into dazzling black stars. My grip tightens on the knife.

'She was teaching him English.'

'What?'

'My mother.' I drop the knife into the sink with a clatter and turn to face him, my hands dripping suds on the floor. 'She was giving him fucking English lessons – nothing else – so he could get a job anywhere but *here*!' I spit that last word in his face. Something shifts behind his eyes.

'And you believe that?'

'As it happens, I've just had a very interesting conversation with Piotr. He told me lots of things you'd probably rather I didn't know.'

Dad's smile is tight-lipped. I can't work out whether this news has unsettled him or not. He tries a different tack.

'Do you know what happens when a gypsy dies?'

'My mother wasn't a gypsy, if that's what you're getting at. The Smiths are show people.'

'Bullshit. Some of Shelby's crew still roam the country laying drives and trotting ponies through town centres.'

'And this from the King of the Scrappies?'

He wants to slap me again, I can tell, but he wants even more to torment me with words.

'The old ones, they burn the deceased's wagon and all their possessions with it. Like a funeral pyre. A warrior's possessions being sent with him to the afterlife.'

'Or her. Warriors can be female.'

'Whatever. The point is' – he strokes his beard like a magistrate about to impart some great judgement – 'if you step out of line once more, or if I catch you where you shouldn't be, I will take your mother's car off you and I will load it with everything that she held most dear.' His menacing stare makes his meaning clear. 'And I will send it to the yard and I will fucking crush it.'

My insides turn to water. He goes to the table and sweeps up the Irn-Bru can, and as our eyes lock in a death grip, he squeezes it in his fist. Liquid dribbles down his wrist like blood. I tear my gaze away, turn back to the sink. I'm shaking. The crushed can sails over my shoulder and lands with a plop in the washing-up water. Greasy spray splashes my face.

I daren't move a muscle to wipe it away, but my father's mood changes abruptly. Whistling, he checks his watch.

'Now, my routine has been well and truly disrupted, but you can make my milky coffee and we'll say no more about it. Good girl.'

26

I hover anxiously by my bedroom window, waiting for Shelby to return. When I hear the familiar growl of his Land Rover, I have to remind myself to appear calm and stay quiet. Downstairs, the door to the sitting room is closed, but I can hear the dull roar of some sports commentary on the TV. The kitchen is empty, yet I find myself tiptoeing.

Opening the back door, I run across the yard to rattle on the caravan door.

'Shel! Open up!'

There's a rumbling and a muffled curse from inside. The door creaks open. 'Where's the fire?'

He seems a bit irritated, and I wonder again where he's been. Waving me in, he slams the door behind me and gestures to the table at the front end, between its two parallel bunks. The windows are all steamy, the velvet curtains half drawn. I slide into the nearest seat. As a child, I remember curling up on this bench, breathing in the familiar scent of damp and bacon fat, lulled by the soft rise and fall of grown-up conversation, usually between Shelby and Mum. Even then, I longed to fall asleep to the rattle and sway of a moving van, to wake up somewhere far from here. There'd be trickling water and lots of green, and always Mum would be there.

'Shel, I have so much to tell you. Oh, I don't even know where to start.' I slide along the bench, tucking myself into the familiar corner. A half-empty mug of tea and a packet of crisps sit on a vinyl mat in the centre of the table. 'Is that your dinner? Crisps?'

'Steak and onion.' He points out. 'Want a brew?'

I turn my nose up at the tan dregs in his cup. 'Pass. Listen, I've just had a run in with Dad.'

'So what's new?'

'He's threatening to crush Mum's car with me in it.'

Shelby makes a little noise. I can tell he's shocked. 'He said those very words?'

'No, not those very words. He threatened to put "everything she held dear" in the car and crush it. But that's his style, isn't it? He damages whatever happens to be closest to you, to make you cry inside.'

I've broken rank, exposed the sullied underbelly of the Rook clan. Shelby shuffles into the seat opposite me and we both stare intently at the crisp packet. Neither of us knows what to say. This is new ground.

Shelby clears his throat. 'Empty words, my love. He'd not do that.'

'In some places they throw the relatives on the funeral pyre. It's kind of the same!' It's all starting to bubble up now – the rage, the fear. Emotions long supressed are worming their way to the surface. 'Did she ever tell you about the car boot? You know he shut her in a fucking car boot overnight?'

Shelby rocks back in his seat, and his voice comes out all quiet and crushed. 'No. No, I did not know that. When was this? I knew she wasn't happy, but . . .'

'When I was sixteen. I'd gone down to the woods with Liam Duthie, and— Oh, it's a long story, but he was so pissed off with me, he went for my mother. Don't you see? That's what he does. What he's always done. Don't tell me it's empty words.'

There's silence between us. My unspoken fear is hovering around me. Why can't I speak up, share my anxieties, get help? I'm angry with myself. Shelby doesn't know what to say, and I want to lash out, to get a reaction. 'He called her a gypsy, and he said that's what they do with a gypsy's possessions when they die.'

He spits out some curse, whether because of the insult or the threat I can't tell. I want to ask him why the hell he's stayed here all these years – an underpaid spanner monkey, forsaking his own country and his wandering genes, subject to my father's whims and moods like the rest of us. He could have upped sticks and left at any time. Was it money or loyalty that kept him here? And what will he do, now that she's gone?

Like the inside of the caravan, he looks old and worn and tired, and my heart sags a little. Over the years, we've shown our affection for each other in a hundred daft little ways. I knock off his hat, he ruffles my hair – that kind of thing. Now I break another rule. I reach for his hand.

'I can't stay here,' I whisper, gripping his fist. 'I need to get away.'

He looks down at my fingers, then opens his palm and squeezes them, in a way he's never done before. I can feel his fear.

'You'll have to wait till the rozzers move off. It'll look strange else, my love.'

'I know. I know.' I draw in a shaky breath. I can't let go of his hand. 'I – I can't leave River here, not without Mum to protect him.'

'He's near a grown man. He can put his wheels down wherever he chooses, and if he chooses not to stay here . . .'

'But he's still at school, *supposedly*. And what about you? You'll be here all alone.'

'Same deal, my love. Maybe I'll take to the road again. But for now . . .'

'We hold the line.' I shoot him a weak smile. 'Yes, I know, but I'm counting the days until I can get on that plane.'

Shelby seems about to say something else, but he stops mid sentence, lets go of my hand and narrows his eyes at the window. 'Isn't that young Rocky? Thought he'd a day off today. What's he doing here?'

I can't stop my heart giving a little kick when I see Piotr. I twist in my seat to get a better view. He is hovering outside the front door, his battered bike leaning against the wall. When I knock on the window, he looks alarmed, but Shelby is already opening the caravan door and ushering him inside.

'There'll be questions asked if the boss sees you,' Shelby mutters, and I wonder if he's seen a flicker of something in my face. There's a moment of awkward shuffling in the confined space and Piotr comes to sit opposite me as Shelby fills the kettle at the tiny sink.

I'm unprepared for the spark that kindles when I finally look Piotr in the eye. It arrests my breath and I'm pretty sure he feels it too. His hands are between us on the table. I want to touch him, but not in the same way I touched Shelby. I sit on my own hands to stop myself.

'I thought you might have spoken to your father. I just wanted to make sure you were . . . safe.'

Over at the stove, Shelby moves slowly. He lights the gas with practised movements. I know he's listening. He's not stupid. He spends his whole life watching and listening.

'I went to see Piotr today,' I explain. 'We had a conversation that shed light on a few things.'

'I'm sorry. I should have told you before.' Piotr looks miserable.

Cold presses in on me. I can't look at him. 'Tell him, Piotr. Tell Shelby what you told me.'

Shelby sets a mug of tea in front of Piotr with a heavy clunk. When he speaks, his voice holds a warning note. 'What exactly is going on?'

'There are things you don't know about me,' Piotr begins. 'In my country, I have a degree in IT.'

Shelby screws up his eyes. 'I thought you were a mechanic? Julie said you were.'

Piotr is shaking his head. 'I know my way around a car. But I also know my way around a motherboard. I was desperate for work when I came here. I'd been picking fruit, but when that came to an end, they told me about the scrappie. Lawler took me on. When he found out about my degree, he thought it would be – what is the word – handy.'

'My father likes people who are handy for him.' My voice sounds hollow.

'The boss, he needed a few things done. He has a lot of . . . deals that are not recorded. He has a deal with me too, which no one knows about.'

'A deal? What are you talking about?' asks Shelby.

'One day, he approached me, asked me what I knew about tracking vehicles. He wanted me to set up a system. Many businesses have it. You attach sensors to the vehicles and track them on your IT system.'

'And you were happy to oblige, weren't you?' I say.

He nods slowly. 'I put tracking devices on all the vehicles, linked to your father's computer. He knows where everyone is, all of the time.'

'So now when my father's on his laptop, or his iPhone, he can see where my mother's car is.' I hold up my hands to Shelby in frustrated disbelief.

'For fuck's sake!' Shelby sweeps a hand through his hair and turns away. Standing there, with his back to us and his hand on his head, it's like he's in pain and he can't move.

'That's how he knew I was at the beach this morning.' My mind slips to that heated exchange in the kitchen, my inside-out T-shirt. 'And there's more. Go on, Piotr.'

'He asked me to clone her mobile.'

'What? What does that mean?' Shelby swings back to us. His eyes are glittering.

'It's not difficult. You just need a hack code to find out the electronic serial number. I put the cloned SIM into a handset for your father, allowing him to receive everything that came to Imelda's phone. Messages, images, every text and call your mother received – it all went to his phone too.'

'For fuck's sake!'

'Shelby! Calm down. She knew. Mum knew. She stopped using her phone. That's why she started calling me from the cafe instead.'

'So how did she know it was cloned?' Shelby demands.

'I told her.' Piotr holds his gaze steadily. 'I didn't want to do this to her. You must believe me.' He turns his attention to me, and his grey eyes soften.

'Even for Lawler, this is extreme.' Shelby looks rattled. 'But I don't understand . . . Why now?'

'He thought Mum was having an affair.'

Shelby digs his fingers into his hair. 'Why would he think that?'

'How would I know?' says Piotr. 'He does not confide in anyone, and he trusts no one. He tells people what to do – that is all I really know about Lawler Rook.'

'But he told you he thought she was cheating on him?' Shelby urges. He's standing at the end of the table, fingers pressed against the edge. 'With who?'

'I do not know.'

'He suspects Piotr. He knew I was at the beach today,' I add, when Piotr looks at me questioningly. 'He was angry. Said my mother spent too much time with you.'

'No,' says Piotr. 'I already told you, she helped me with my English, so I could get a better job here. We were friends, nothing more.'

'Friends?' I repeat. 'How could you do that to her, if you were friends?'

'I had no choice. He threatened me, said that if I did not do this for him – put trackers on the vehicles and clone the phone – I would . . .'

'What?' This time I do reach for him. I want to believe him, to trust him. His dimple appears briefly, but it's more of a nervous tic.

'He said Offshore Dave would pay me a visit. He said lots of foreign nationals get washed up on the beach, but nobody cares and their bodies get shipped back to their families with no questions asked.'

'Shit.' Shelby and I exchange a look.

Piotr is one of us – both victim and collaborator.

27

Piotr leaves the caravan not long after that. He has no good reason for being here and he doesn't want to risk running into my father. I don't blame him. I've spent my whole life wandering around with reasons and excuses on the tip of my tongue, just in case. Shelby has folded in on himself and barely mutters a goodbye, so it's left to me to show Piotr out. I want to squeeze his shoulder, make contact, but I'm scared of giving myself away. Once outside, he turns and looks at me, and I realise that he already knows how I feel. Truth shimmers between us, and it's hotter than any physical touch.

Now he's gone, riding the wobbly bike with a torch strapped to the handle bars, and I stand braced in the doorway, watching the light disappear.

'Are you in or out?' Shelby grunts. 'You're letting in the cold.'

'Sorry.' I close the door gently. 'Shel, there's more stuff too. It's River. He won't talk to me. He's hiding something. You know my mother called social services about him?' This is the trouble with confiding in people. Once you start, it's hard to stop. I don't know why I haven't confided in Shelby before. Everything seemed stuck; knotted up inside me. 'And the money. Do you know about the money?'

Shelby lowers his brows at me. 'That's an awful lot of questions all at once.'

Without his hat, he seems older, less significant, and I realise – for the first time – that maybe he doesn't have all the answers. I grew up thinking he knew everything, that he had a well of secret knowledge way down deep, but now I see he's frail, just getting by like the rest of us, and I feel bad for hectoring him.

'How are you doing, Shel?'

'Oh, holding the line. That's all we can do. Keep our nerve.'

I reach for his hand again, and we stay like that for a moment, standing together in the gloom of the caravan.

'It isn't my money.'

Shelby is wearing that closed look, the one he adopts when he doesn't want to answer awkward questions. My head is starting to hurt from thinking about it all, and I let out a huge sigh.

'Look, I'd better go. It's been quite a day, with one thing and another. I'm knackered.'

'Before you go . . .' Shelby holds out his arms and I find myself in his embrace. The surprises keep on coming. He has never done this, and now it's like he doesn't want to let me go. I bury my face in the softness of his shirt. For the briefest of moments, I feel safe, like nothing can touch me, but he prises me away and holds me at arm's length.

'Promise me you'll leave – as soon as you're able, my love. Don't be like your mother. She wasted all that energy on a situation that couldn't be altered. There's been too much time wasted.'

He looks like he wants to say more, but even though the words are hovering close to the surface, he clamps his lips shut.

'I promise.' I'm suddenly scared. Things are changing in unexpected ways. I lay my hand on Shelby's shoulder. It's thin and frail beneath his soft plaid shirt. Too much time wasted.

I go upstairs to the bathroom and lock myself in. Running the shower until the water steams, I climb into the cubicle. It's the smallest space in the house, the equivalent of curling up in a corner and drawing a blanket over my head. I'm finally paying attention to my memories, my flashbacks, my mother's veiled hints – all the danger signs that I'd chosen to ignore for so long.

We've been living in denial – Mum, River, Shelby, me. Complicit. But I can't afford to push my father too far. He knows I'm onto him, and I need to get out of here in one piece.

The shower is stocked with cheap toiletries. He would never let my mother splash the cash on good quality brands. He'd give her just enough money to buy cheap shit, and then he'd check the receipts. I never knew that until my last visit, when I opened a drawer and found a treasure trove of birthday presents I'd sent her: Miss Dior perfume, Lush body butter – high-end cosmetics I'd really wanted to keep for myself. I suppose on some level I'd been compensating for all the nice things my father should have lavished on her but never did. We'd had a row about the stuff in the drawer – life is too short to keep things for best, I'd argued. But it wasn't that, she'd said. He'd think she'd bought fancy stuff and lied to him. I'd told her not to be so silly. It was easy for me to jet off, leaving her to cajole and appease him. Why hadn't I listened more to the space between her words? She had no escape; she had to live with him, always following the path of least resistance.

I choose a budget shower gel that smells of lime, and I soap my body. The sensation reminds me of Piotr, the way my skin must have felt to his touch, the way he made me lose myself for a little while. I gave myself up to what happened in his bed, a makeshift, ill-timed coming together of bodies, but my mind stayed out of it, alert but unmoved. The thought makes me sad. I longed to be moved by Piotr. In another time, perhaps. In another place. He fascinates me, a bright flame against the grey North Sea, but sex shouldn't have been part of the equation. No baggage, no strings, no regret – he makes me long for my backpacker life. He is foreignness and freedom. A reminder. Maybe we're all gypsies deep down, happier without roots.

But I do have roots. Sooner or later I'm going to have to deal with what's been going on here. Panic begins to gnaw at my insides. I'd fooled myself into thinking this was a visit – under tragic circumstances, obviously, but still just a visit. Instead, I've walked into a hornet's nest.

I no longer smell of the sea, or of Piotr. I'm washed clean. A part of me doesn't want to let him go so easily. I want to cling on to the dark space we generated between us, filled with soft words, caresses, kindness. A creeping dread has taken hold inside me like a stubborn stain.

Wrapping myself in the biggest towel I can find, I perch, be-turbaned and shivering, on the edge of the bath. I don't know what's going to happen next. A drip of water slides down my cheek like a tear.

That night, I sleep very badly and wake up in the middle of another car cemetery dream. I think I hear the noise of an engine in the yard, and I suddenly remember the box that Offshore Dave keeps, filled with stuff that he's salvaged from cars about to be crushed: spectacles and scarves, cuddly toys and tins of travel sweets. As a child, the wrecked cars that came into the yard scared the shit out of me; they seemed wounded, vulnerable. Imagine leaving home, full of purpose and in high spirits, and hours later you're a mangled wreck being towed up the drive. I never thought of the people that were mangled and broken – it was always the cars. Once Dave found a severed thumb and chased me round the yard with it, until Julie hit him with a broom handle. I was about eight. No wonder my dreams are always full of phantom vehicles.

The border between dreaming and waking is hazy, and when I wake up for a second time, it's morning.

28

Fourteen Days After

I wander through the empty house with a new wariness in my step. I haven't heard my father in the bathroom and he's not sitting at the table with his porridge. The kettle is stone cold. After yesterday's confrontation, it seems safest to avoid him. The sensation of being choked comes back to me on a wave of panic, and I ease my fingers under the neckline of my top. As I set about making my breakfast, I try to think of other things, to recapture the feeling of safety I felt in Shelby's embrace. Maybe together we can begin to make things right. I could get him to have a word with River, man to man.

As the kettle grumbles to the boil, I wander over to the window. It's still half dark out there, and it's wet. On the window pane, a fine cobweb of raindrops sparkles in the yard lights. I'm just wondering what's tripped the motion sensor when I hear the low growling of a dog. I realise Dave's van is already parked up in the yard, much earlier than usual. If I press my nose to the glass, I can just make out his elbow and the bushy tail of one of the German shepherds.

Prickling with unease, I let myself softly out the back door. Dave has the dogs tightly leashed and they start up a frantic barking as soon as they see me. They bear no resemblance to the fluffy pups I once held in my arms. My father is out there too, standing over by the fence, staring at the ground. Something is different, and I struggle for a moment to work out what it is.

The last fragments of that safe feeling dissolve like a dream. Shelby's caravan is gone. My father is standing on a dry, discoloured, caravan-shaped vacancy.

'What the fuck is he playing at? What the fuck? Did you know about this?' Dad's glaring at me, and I can only shake my head. How could he leave without a word? My throat begins to knot with tears. This feels like the last straw.

Dad is predictably furious, but there's something else: Shelby has abandoned his beaten-up Land Rover Defender and taken off with my father's gleaming white Range Rover. River emerges from the house behind me. He's hunched against the rain, in pyjama bottoms, his arms folded across his bare torso. A sprinkling of chest hair reminds me of the man he is becoming. Like the dogs, no longer cute and cuddly, but another male force to be reckoned with.

'Shelby's gone,' I say, unnecessarily. Dad is barking the same question at my brother, and River's saying no, he doesn't know anything either.

'Why would he take your wheels?'

Dad is circling on the spot in disbelief. I think we're all waiting for the explosion.

'I was only speaking to him yesterday evening,' I put in quickly. 'He never said a word.'

'How bloody dare he? Without even a nod?' Dad stops his pivoting and crosses the yard so swiftly that I jump when his face juts into mine. Water is dripping off his eyelashes, his beard. His blue eyes lance through me and leave me shivering. 'I bet you know something about this.'

'No, I don't. I swear it.' My hand flutters around my neck, and my stomach clamps in on itself. 'It's a total shock to me too.'

Why hadn't Shelby said something? All that talk about wasted time – what was he trying to tell me? Leaving Dad and River and Dave to discuss the theft of the Range Rover, I withdraw quietly back into the kitchen. Of course he took Dad's car.

He knew it would be the only vehicle that wasn't fitted with a tracking device. Shelby doesn't want to be found.

An idea is beginning to form. A possibility. I go to the fridge and haul open the freezer compartment, urgent fingers digging out the margarine tub marked 'Lentil soup'. The lid is loose; the cash is missing. The door bangs and the men troop in.

'Make some tea and bacon rolls, Ellie. There's a good girl.'

I hear work boots stomping over the tiles and chairs being scraped back, but I don't respond. My eyes are fixed on the empty plastic box. *It isn't my money.*

'Ellie, did you hear me?'

'Yes, Dad.' I shove the box back into the fridge and swing the door shut. River catches my eye.

'All these years! All these fucking years – rent free!' Dad bangs his fists on the table and the dogs growl. 'I'm a spanner-man down and a vehicle short, and not so much as a by your leave!'

Dave shakes his head. 'A-fucking-palling. He needs to be taught a lesson, boss.'

'Damn fucking right he does.'

I put the kettle on, take out the big black frying pan. 'I'll just see if your paper's been delivered, Dad.'

I make a face at River and he catches on quick, meeting me in the hall. We huddle together out of earshot of the closed kitchen door.

'This isn't good,' River whispers. 'Shelby's fucked. What was he thinking, taking the Range Rover?'

I explain about the tracking devices in a rushed whisper, watching the door like it's a snake about to strike. River stares at me in disbelief.

'Rocky? You're kidding.'

I pull him closer to the front door, away from the kitchen. 'It's true. Dad forced Piotr to fix devices to all the vehicles. He can track everyone just by checking his phone. When I was parked up at the beach yesterday, he knew exactly where I was, and for how long.' My hand strays once again to my throat. 'River, he guessed I was with Piotr yesterday. He tried to choke me and he . . . he threatened me.'

'What? He's upset, because of Mum. He doesn't mean anything by it.'

'Don't do that!' I want to shake him. 'Don't make excuses for him. He tried to fucking throttle me!'

'Shh! He'll hear.' River looks uncertain. He's torn between what he thinks he knows and the ugly truth. I press home my point.

'He's a fucking control freak. Remember Mum stopped using her mobile? Cloned.'

'Cloned?'

I open my mouth to tell him more, but the ding-dong of the front doorbell makes us both leap. I unlock the front door a crack, wearing my *not today* scowl, but it's Sharon, with Liam lurking behind her. He's hunched in a thin jacket, shoulders dark with rain. She's wielding a green umbrella and obviously on a mission.

'Ellie! I thought I'd pop by just to see. I saw your dad leaving in the middle of the night and wondered if they'd found her, your mum?' I open my mouth to say it wasn't Dad driving the Range Rover, but she rattles on. 'I was up all night. I made a shepherd's pie and I thought the mince smelled a bit funny, and I was right. It gave me the runs. I reckon that's what did it. Couldn't get off the toilet. I was just opening the bathroom window, and I leaned out to get a bit of air and I saw the white car stopped on the drive and your dad opening the gate. Well, I just went and shouted at Liam. "Wake up! They must have had a call. From the police."'

'I was asleep,' Liam grunts. 'I told her you'd let us know if there's any news.'

He looks like he'd rather be anywhere else than standing on our doorstep in the rain. I haven't replied to any of his texts since the day we went down to the beach, and it looks like he's in the huff, Sharon hasn't mentioned the caravan – from her bathroom window, in the dark, the chances are she only caught a glimpse of a shadowy figure opening the gate and assumed it was my father. I don't want to start a discussion about Shelby, but the kitchen door bursts open and Dad appears.

'Sharon!' He shakes her warmly by the hand, causing her to juggle with the brolly and nearly poke Liam in the eye with one of the spokes. 'Thanks for coming over. Your support means such a lot. On this occasion it was a false alarm.'

'Oh.' She looks unreasonably disappointed.

Dad begins to close the door. 'Thanks again. We'll let you know.'

'Ellie, I'll call you.' Liam raises his voice, but the door slams, and the last thing I see is Sharon's disappointed face and rain bouncing off the umbrella.

'Right, you two. We need to go. Forget the damn breakfast, Ellie. River, go and get dressed. We have things to do.'

River takes the stairs two at a time, and I follow Dad into the kitchen. The back door is standing open, and I can see Dave loading the dogs into the van. My father is scrolling on his phone. Surely he can't be tracking his own vehicle? I experience a little prod of alarm. Where are you, Shelby? *Stay safe*. When I place a mug of tea in front of Dad, he looks up briefly.

'You are not to leave the house, understand? And you can give me your phone. I don't want anyone tipping him off.'

'Shelby doesn't have a mobile.'

'So? You two have always been as thick as thieves. I'm sure you'll come up with a way to get a message to him. Phone.' I slide it out of my back pocket and slam it down so hard on the table it almost cracks. He shoots me a look. 'I don't trust you. You've always been a sneaky bitch, keepings things from me. You take after your mother.'

'If I took after my mother I'd have fucking drowned myself too!'

His hand flies out without warning. The sting of his slap radiates through me and I stagger back. I grab a chair, nursing my cheek, but when I look up, he's taking my phone over to the sink. I hear a plop.

'No!'

I hurl myself after him to find my mobile sinking to the bottom of the full washing-up bowl. He's chuckling to himself as he leaves.

'River, get in the back.'

'No, River, don't go!'

I cling to his arm, and although he shakes me off, he makes no move forward. I know this River – the pale, shy little boy peeping out of the man's body. I grip his arm again. *Don't do it*, my eyes plead with him.

'Get in the fuckin' van.' Dad isn't prepared to mess about. Offshore Dave is holding the door open with a mocking smile. I hear him say, 'Want a leg up, milady?' as River climbs into the front, and I'm suddenly more afraid for him than I've ever been in my life. I need to get him out of here – away from this place, this life. He needs to find himself, like I attempted to do. I almost managed it, but the scrappie has put a spanner in the works. I'm no longer Ellie Rook; I'm the ghost of Imelda, waiting for Lawler Rook to return from whatever nefarious, macho business he's been conducting. Waiting for River to turn into the same sort of man.

As the van pulls away in a haze of burning oil, I drag my feet back into the kitchen. I find a bag of rice in the cupboard and pop the waterlogged phone into it, and then I wander around the kitchen, wiping surfaces and generally trying to occupy myself. My stomach is churning so much I feel like I'm going to throw up. My gaze travels over the sink, the cooker, the plastic washing basket piled with blue boiler suits, towels, boxer shorts. The table with its crumbs and plates that no one else will bother to clean.

A white mist is rising up to meet me. I pick up Dad's 'World's Greatest Boss' mug and drop it. The resulting crash is so satisfying I turn to the dresser and Grandma Rook's precious wedding china. The plates sit bolt upright like Edwardian ladies in pink flowered silk. I take them off, one at a time, and smash them to the floor. One for Mum, one for River, one for Shelby, one for me: all the people who have been kept prisoner in this house, bound by *his* ways and *his* rules. Crockery tumbles from the shelves with a noise that makes my heart shrink, but I cannot stop. I find his pathetic little pot of mustard in the cupboard. I unscrew the top and put my fingers in and calmly smear it all over the blue boiler suits. That's for all those years of keeping him clean, Mum. All those years of not revealing the dirty secret of abuse to the world.

I'm giggling like a little kid, but there's a fine line between laughter and tears. My hysteria turns into big ugly sobs. I stand in the middle of the kitchen and take a last look at my handiwork, but the scene is a blur. Grabbing Mum's car keys, I leave, slamming the door behind me.

29

I scramble into the car without any clear idea of where I'm going, but it no longer matters. He'll know where I am. Sweat creeps up my spine; my back is hot and sticky against the driver's seat. Mum's little koala dances a jig beneath the mirror as I swing erratically onto the drive. The Fiesta bounces over the ruts, front wheels spinning on mud as I nose out onto the road.

Liam is in his front garden, testing the hinges on the gate, toing and froing it, giving it a test jiggle. I wonder if he's waiting for me, and when he glances up there's a shadow of disappointment on his face. There is no escape. I slow to a crawl and open the window.

'Remember that end-of-term party when I crashed into this gate on Danny Findlater's new moped? It's never been the same since.'

He's trying to draw me in with his nostalgia game, but I no longer want to play. My memories are not rose-tinted and I'm sick of pretending. I glare at the gate.

'No longer fit for purpose,' I mutter.

He gives me a surly look. 'Must try and get it fixed.' He closes the gate with a click. 'Where are you off to?'

I shrug. 'No idea. I just need to get away for a bit.'

He flicks ash from his cigarette into the hedge. His mother doesn't let him smoke in the house, because of her chest. 'Is everything . . . Are you okay? Your Dad was a bit weird when we called. I told Mum not to interfere, but—'

'It's fine. Everything's fine.'

'You got time for a coffee? Mum's away to the hairdressers.'

'Jesus.' I grip the steering wheel and stare straight ahead. 'It's like going back in time.'

'What?'

I glare at him through the open window. 'Us two, creeping around. Waiting for the grown-ups to disappear.'

'I didn't mean that!' Liam looks genuinely aggrieved, and I experience a flash of guilt.

'I'm sorry. I know you didn't, but I . . . I'm dealing with a very grown-up situation here.'

He lifts the latch and opens the gate a fraction. 'Come in and tell me about it.'

He's too close. Too close to the old me and too close to home. I need to keep driving, keep running, so that nothing can stick. I rev the engine a little. 'Not now. I can't.'

The window glides to a close and I jam down the accelerator. His injured expression fills my wing mirror; I watch his familiar slouch grow small and disappear. The vague sense of guilt is harder to shake off.

I start speaking the moment Piotr opens his dilapidated door. I'd only realised I was heading for him when I parked my car on the clifftop. It seemed to make sense.

'I need to know – Dad's Range Rover, does it have a tracking device? Shelby's done a runner and he's taken Dad's car instead of his own.'

He shakes his head. 'No. Why would he track his own vehicle? Come in.'

I'm sure he could do without me and my drama, but, polite as ever, he keeps his face neutral and steps aside to let me pass. I'm wobbling inside, like my organs are coming loose and will never work properly again. Especially my heart. I want my heart to be kind and generous, to trust, to fall in love. First Mum, then Shelby and now River. My heart is a mangled mess and I don't think I can hurt any more than I do now.

Instinctively I head for the fire, sloughing off my jacket, but the chair is festooned with washing. There's a pleasant laundry fug in the air, and I note Piotr's freshly washed socks are draped over the log pile. One of them has a hole in the toe, and it tugs at me in a way I don't understand. The single red glove is sitting beside them, and I pick it up and squeeze my hand inside.

'How can one man fuck up so many people?' I flex blood-red fingers at the fire.

Piotr comes up behind me and pulls off the glove. He wraps his fingers around mine.

'He's got River,' I whisper. 'He's taken that poor boy to do his dirty work.'

Piotr drops my hand and puts his arms around me. I bury my cheek against his jumper and we stand, swaying slightly, as if we're on a boat. The soft swell and swoosh of the sea whispers in the chimney. It's a comfort, a bit like I'd experienced with Shelby, but not quite. Piotr is still an unknown quantity. From here I can see his bed, and something nudges through all the bad feelings, takes me back to that one time I let him in. Suddenly I notice an open rucksack, all his clothes piled on the sleeping bag. *Boom.*

I jerk my head upright. 'What's this? Not you as well?'

He's still holding me. He sees where I'm looking but his eyes are fixed on my face. He won't let go. 'I'm going back to Poland. I'm done with Lawler Rook. Come with me. You can't stay here. Not now.'

I'm thinking of the trashed kitchen and the broken china and the mustard, but I guess he's thinking of my mother. *Nothing to stay for*, that's what he's saying.

'There are things I have to do,' I say carefully. 'Loose ends. I need to tie them up before I can begin again.'

'Begin again with me. I mean it.'

I pull myself gently from his arms. 'I know you do. But not yet. Not yet.'

'What are you waiting for?'

I'm still not sure how far I can trust him. I jerk my head towards the socks. 'Don't pack them damp,' I say. 'They'll be stinking by the time you get where you're going.'

It's all I can give him for now. It makes him smile, but then he turns deadly serious.

'Ellie, wait – did Shelby take the caravan?'

'Yeah. Just upped sticks and left. But they'll not find him, will they? Shelby knows the wild places. He'll hide the caravan and—'

'Ellie, the caravan has a tracking sensor on it.'

30

The sign on the cafe door is flipped to 'Closed' even though it's still early afternoon. I'd texted River using Piotr's mobile and we'd arranged to meet me here. Now alarm twists through me. I try the door, but it's locked. Shading my eyes, I peer through the glass. The place is empty, but I can make out Ned, rummaging through a box on one of the tables. The interior of the cafe is gloomy, but two things hit me: the box is a first aid kit; and there is River, sitting at the table with his head in his hands.

'Oh Jesus.' I rattle the door. Ned reacts quickly, crossing the space in a few strides to let me in. I race to my brother's side, and grip his wrists. 'Show me. What has he done?'

Ned is ripping the wrapper from a gauze swab. 'It's not pretty. They got back twenty minutes ago, and River insisted they drop him off in the village.'

River raises his head slowly. All I can see is dried blood – crusting under his nose, around his lips. One cheek is shiny and swollen, and his eye is half closed. He looks like he's been crying. I fight down rising nausea.

River whispers something. I have to lean in to catch it. 'I don't want to go home.'

I swallow. 'That's why I said to come here. I don't know where else to go.'

'Your father is an animal.' Ned glares at me, as if it's my fault, and douses the swab with wound spray. 'I'm just going to look after that lip.'

I take a step back, listening to Ned's sing-song words of comfort and the occasional 'ouch' from River. It was always me who looked after him. Now Ned is between us, blocking my view with his broad back, and I try to quell a sudden burst of resentment. I tell myself to stop. Maybe Ned will protect him in a way I cannot. I failed him. I attacked the house when I should have been attacking that monster. I should have done that long ago.

Should have. I should have. Should. Should . . .

The words pulse in my brain like song lyrics. Ned steps back to admire his ministrations. 'All done. You'll have to put your film career on hold for a while, but you'll live.'

I push past him to wrap my arms around River and hug him awkwardly, making him wince. 'What did he do to you? What happened?'

'He needs locking up,' Ned growls. 'Seriously. We need to call the police.'

River and I exchange a look. We're Rooks. No police.

'Dad was able to track the caravan. They drove to the exact spot.' River forms the words gingerly, wincing on the 's' sound. His bottom lip is split and swollen. 'Shelby had taken a forestry track, up in the hills. The caravan was hidden in the trees.' Images of fists and snarling dogs crowd my head, and I squeeze his shoulder. He recoils. I'm not sure if he's hurting on the outside or the inside.

'I can't get it out of my head – Offshore banging on the caravan door. When Shel opened up, he grabbed him by the shirt, hauled him out. His hat fell off. I can still see him in the dirt, with Dave kicking him down every time he got up.'

No. Oh no. I might have said it out loud. As River's voice breaks, Ned pulls up a chair and takes hold of his hand. I notice the redness and bruising around my brother's knuckles.

'Go on.' My voice sounds broken too. I'm not sure I want to hear this.

River sniffs noisily. 'I tried to get to him, to make it stop, but Dad held me back. When I shook him off, he did this.' He touches his face gingerly. 'I ended up grappling with Dad, and when I looked again, Shel was lying on the ground – totally still.'

'Oh my God. Is he— Was he breathing?' My hands fly to my throat.

'I don't know. Dad decided to drive the Range Rover back, but while Dave was loading the dogs in the back of the van, I was able to call 999. I thought that, even if I didn't speak, the ambulance people would be able to trace my call, but Dave heard the operator on the other end and threatened to tell Dad. I stuck the phone in my pocket, but I didn't disconnect the call.'

'Good. That's good,' says Ned. 'They'll have traced the call, sent help.'

'Where will they take him?' I jump up. 'Where will they take Shelby? We need to go to him.'

'The hospital in Aberdeen.'

'I'll phone. Can I use your phone?'

'What happened to yours?' River says.

'It drowned. I tried some rice-based therapy, but . . .' I shrug.

They both look at me like I've taken leave of my senses, and then Ned whips out his iPhone. 'Here. And phone the police while you're at it. Report your father. For all we know, he's wanted for fucking murder.'

I go outside to make the call – to the hospital, not the police. I'm still a Rook, after all. The woman I speak to puts me on hold for a very long time, until she eventually returns with zero information. She suggests I call the police. I disconnect her in mid sentence and begin to pace rapidly up and down, pressing the phone to my mouth, until Ned comes out and takes it from me. He surreptitiously checks it for teeth marks before slipping it into his back pocket.

'No news then?'

I don't answer. Thoughts are whirring around in my head. Why there, Shelby? Why didn't you get the hell away from here, take off down south? Why did you let yourself be cornered at the end of a mountain track?

Ignoring Ned, I barge back into the cafe and confront River, who is still slumped over the table.

'Did you contact the hospital?' he says. 'Is there any news?'

'Was Shelby alone, River?'

He scowls at me, tries to shake the question away with a painful movement of his head. 'Of course he was alone.'

'Did you look? Did you see anything . . . strange?'

'What are you talking about? There wasn't exactly time for a tour.'

'River, can you take me to the caravan? Do you remember where you went?'

He nods. I glance at Ned, who is pretending to rearrange the menus on a neighbouring table. I have a moment of sympathy for him. He doesn't know what to do, caught up in the middle of all this family drama. He gives a shrug and disappears into the kitchen to give us some privacy.

'Of course I can find it,' River says. 'It's the place we used to go as kids. Mum used to take us to the hills, remember?'

I remember. 'Let's go. I'll explain on the way.'

Sitting in the car, we manage to pinpoint the location of the caravan on Google Maps.

'It was right up on the top of a hill,' River says. 'A real climb. Offshore was cursing the bends. He said . . .' His face sags as he remembers what happened when they got to the top. He's grown up with both Offshore Dave and Shelby in his life. We both know there's no coming back from this.

'Anyway,' he continues. 'Here's the forest, woods, whatever. It's pretty dense, and we ended up on that track we used to call the Road to Nowhere.'

I take the phone from him, zoom in on the spot.

'I remember. Where the forestry stops, the hills begin. You can see in every direction from the top. An entire kingdom, Mum used to say. A whole lot cleaner than Lawler Rook's kingdom. There are some weird ridges up there – piles of stones under the grass. It's said to be the site of Finella's castle. Mum certainly thought it was. Said she had a connection with the place.' I hand back the phone and our eyes meet. 'River, Shelby took that money.'

'What? The stash in the soup tub? Was it his?'

I shake my head and start the ignition. 'It wasn't his. Come on, I have a hunch.'

'But the hospital . . . We need to find out how he is.'

'We need to go to the woods first. Trust me.'

River gives me the sort of look that makes him resemble Dad, but I ignore it and put the car into gear. I have a hunch. I hope I'm right.

We climb out of the car like sailors going up on deck: getting our bearings, trying to fix ourselves in this alien landscape. It's cooler up here, the light crowded out by the trees. The scent of pine makes me think of Christmas. A crow starts cawing somewhere high up and out of sight, and I feel myself relax a little. The caravan, so familiar, looks smaller than it did in the yard. River points to something on the ground, just under the van. Shelby's fedora, lying in the dirt, like a stunned bird.

'Did Dad go into the caravan?'

River shrugs. 'He kind of glanced in it after Shel came out.'

'Check the caravan,' I say to him. He looks at me oddly but slopes off, and as he's opening the door, I stoop to retrieve the hat. There's a patch of dried mud on the crown and a sprinkling of pine needles sticking to the dusty felt. Poked into the hatband are a row of blue-black feathers that I've never noticed before.

River steps out of the caravan. 'What am I supposed to be looking for?' He spots me hugging the hat to my chest. 'I saw Dad pick that up, but he chucked it away like he was disgusted with it.'

I turn to face the dimness of the trees, try to slow my breathing. My stomach is churning like a washing machine. 'Maybe I'm totally wrong.'

But I *know*. I just do. As soon as I realised that Shelby had taken off in the night with that money – Mum's money – I knew.

A twig cracks in the woods. I find it hard to pull away, to look in the direction of the noise, because I'm scared it's just the soft, silly fluttering of a pheasant. But River is shaking my arm and *he's* gazing into the trees, and he's smiling.

'So *that's* why he came here! Look!'

I look. A figure is stepping briskly towards us, coat flapping and boots kicking up leaves and twigs as she breaks into a run. Best of all, her arms are open and I'm flying into them. *Run, Finella, run!* My mother catches me in her arms and holds me like she'll never let me go again.

'So, Plan A isn't fucking working,' she says. 'We might need to come up with a Plan B.'

31

'But he didn't see you? No one saw you?'

Mum shakes her head. There's dirt on her face and she looks like she's been sleeping rough. We've taken shelter in the caravan, but without Shelby there it feels all wrong. The familiar smell of bacon and cigarettes still lingers, but his absence is a physical pain. We sit round the table in our coats, like uninvited guests. I've placed Shelby's hat in the centre, but the thought of his head on some hospital pillow makes me want to weep. I reach for my mother's hands across the Formica.

'Jesus, this is the hardest secret I've ever had to keep!' I say, squeezing her cold fingers.

River gives a half laugh. 'What about me? Try keeping a secret like that in the yard! No wonder I'm so fucked up in the head.'

'I had to go along with Liam Duthie's bloody search party – *and* speak to that policewoman!'

'I lied to her too!' River butts in. 'I told everyone I was there at the end. The end that wasn't the fucking end.'

'Hey!' Mum flashes her dark eyes at us, the way she always does when we argue. I hadn't realised we were arguing. It doesn't feel like the right time, although all sorts of things are bubbling to the surface now that we can see her in the flesh. I'm shocked by the resentment I feel, because I've missed her. More than once, I've found myself shedding real tears when Sharon or Julie go all sympathetic and gooey. I have almost believed the lie. But now, face to face . . . What the hell has she gotten us into? I look down at her hands. The skin is rough and there's dirt under her nails. I want to take her home and make everything go back to normal, but then I remember our normal was all wrong.

Her grip on my fingers is painful. 'I was out in the woods when they came. They didn't see me, but I saw them. Doing nothing was the hardest thing I've ever had to do.' Her voice breaks. I release her hands so she can poke around in her coat pockets for a miserable bit of tissue.

'I tried to stop them,' River says. 'Dad smacked me in the mouth.'

His fingers creep to his lips and Mum makes a face. A tear shivers on her eyelashes.

'I saw that too. I don't know how I could let it happen . . . I was so close to getting away with it. I was almost there.'

'You're still there,' I tell her. 'As far as they know, you're still dead.'

We pause for a moment to digest this. Gently, I shake her hands. 'Go on. What happened, after they'd gone?'

She continues, in a voice thick with tears. 'I ran over to him – my poor Shel, all beaten up and limp – and I thought, what the fuck am I going to do now? I don't have a phone. Lawler took his bloody Range Rover back, so I've no transport. What the hell was I supposed to do?'

'I phoned the ambulance,' River puts in quickly. I know he's ashamed that he couldn't do more.

She smiles weakly, showing off the gap between her front teeth that always seemed a bit sassy. Now she just looks sad. 'I tried to bring him round. I thought if I could just get him on his feet, I could get him into the caravan, patch him up, but then I heard the sirens. I had just enough time to tidy him up a bit and take his wallet.' When I narrow my eyes at her, she goes all defensive. 'I had to! He wouldn't want the rozzers poking their noses in, and I couldn't risk the authorities getting in touch with your father. I had to protect him from Lawler. It was the cops first, and then the air ambulance landed on the hill. Poor Shelby was mumbling, so he was kind of conscious, but he wasn't making any sense. I had to leave him . . . It was awful, but I couldn't let myself be found. I hid in the bushes behind the caravan.'

'Oh my God.' I bury my head in my hands.

The enormity of what we've done is beginning to sink in. We're digging a hole that's getting deeper by the minute, and we need to keep up this charade for life. FOR LIFE. I look up suddenly. Shelby had been in on the deception from the beginning, of course, but I never guessed the two of them had been keeping a secret all of their own. Only when Piotr told me about my father's suspicions did I begin to go through the options.

'So how long has this little love affair been going on, under our noses? You've kept it quiet, haven't you? I only put two and two together when Shelby upped sticks. Wagons roll, but his hasn't moved for years.'

'I've known Shelby for ever. Distant cousins and all that,' she says. 'Not related, not really. I love him to bits. I've always loved him. Him moving up here was a way for us to be together. Not the best way, but . . . Well, you know the score.' Her gaze flits between River and me, and we nod in unison. We know the score.

'I've been sleeping up here in a bender,' she says. 'That was part of the plan, so he would know where to find me. I've been saving money for years – stashed it in a soup container in the freezer, so Dad didn't know. I should have taken it with me, but I wasn't sure my plan would work. What if he came after me and found the money? He'd know I was leaving, and he wouldn't let that happen.' Her voice breaks. 'You know that, Ellie. We've always known he'd kill me rather than let me leave.'

For a moment I can't speak. The truth has been let loose, this shameful knowledge known only to us, deep down. Never voiced, never shared. My tongue won't form any words, even though the spell of silence has been broken.

I recover enough to say, 'So Shel brought you the money – your rainy-day dosh. I thought it was River's drug money.'

River raises his eyebrows in such a comical way that I almost laugh. Yes, it's ludicrous that I suspected my brother of dealing drugs, but what was I supposed to think?

Mum shakes her head, as if it's all too much to take in. 'And then it all felt very real. I'd done it. I'd got out of that place.'

I look at her with a sudden flare of irritation. 'You know the dust is never going to settle, right?'

I try and catch her gaze, but she won't let me in.

'You hear about people faking their deaths all the time,' she continues. 'I knew it was the only way I would ever get away from your father. He told me he'd hunt me down and kill me if I left. And that was without knowing about Shelby.'

I sit back and take a good look at her: the deep frown line; the lank hair. Wildwood leaves clinging to her coat. She smells different and dirty. Maybe I did lose her to the waterfall, and she's come back as something else. Not my mother, but someone new. I have no idea what we're going to do next, but somehow I have to come up with an addendum to Plan A.

'Right. You can't stay here. If the cops get fresh info about Shelby, this will turn into a crime scene. They'll be right back – and so will Dad, if he gets an inkling of what's going on.'

'He won't. He thinks I'm dead.'

I'm no longer convinced of anything. Fear cramps my stomach like hunger. 'Get your things together and we'll . . . we'll sort something out.'

'Where are we going to take her?' River asks. 'Remember, Dad could be tracking your car at this very minute.'

'He can try.' I shoot him a sly grin. 'I made Piotr promise to disable the software. Dad won't be tracking anything any more.'

'Good job.' River holds up his fist and I bump it with mine.

I take a deep, shuddery breath. 'I hate to say it, but our jackets are on a very shaky peg. Aiding and abetting a fake death, plus wasting police time, and not to mention getting on the wrong side of Dad.'

'Plan A was a shit plan.' Mum wipes her eyes and I reach for her hands again.

'I've thought of something . . .' I say. 'It just might work, if we can hold our nerve.' Shelby's voice comes to me from a great distance: *Hold the line*. It gives me strength.

'What about Shel?' Mum picks nervously at the feathers on Shelby's hat. 'I put these in his hatband. I've been feeding the crows out in the woods and they bring me little presents. Sticks, stones, feathers.'

'Buttons.' I remember my little black visitor in the sitting room, with his message of hope. 'One thing at a time. We'll get you to a safe place and then we'll worry about Shel. Come on, let's go get your tent and stuff.'

As plans go, it's a precarious one. It will mean walking into the lion's den. And asking my mother to face up to her worst nightmare.

32

It's almost dark by the time we turn into the yard. My stomach is tying itself in knots as I nose the Fiesta between the Range Rover and Offshore Dave's van. What is Dave still doing here? The security lights snap on and the vacant plot of Shelby's caravan shocks me all over again. The yard seems desolate. I cut the engine but neither of us wants to move. River reaches for the door handle with deliberate slowness.

'If this doesn't work . . .'

'It will work.' I refuse to dwell on any other outcome. 'Grit your teeth. We walk in, let him say what he's got to say and I'll take it from there.'

We step out into puddles of soapy water. Offshore Dave has been hosing away the evidence and the two vehicles are glistening down to their tyre treads. So that's why he's here. An orange glow spills from the kitchen window, and I experience the familiar squeeze of fear as I imagine Dad waiting for us. He's probably having his supper – a ham sandwich, perhaps. I wonder if he found the mustard.

River pauses with his hand on the back door. Everything is changing, and it's hard for him. I forget sometimes how young he is. Dad treats him like a man, expects him to behave like a man, and yet he's still a teenager. At fifteen, you don't want to have to think about your parents' relationship. You live in a different world – you close your bedroom door, stick on some loud music and zone out. I've been there. But it comes at a price.

We enter, resisting the urge to cling to each other – the babes in the woods.

Dad is sitting at the table in his usual place. He's tinkering with a vintage Bakelite radio, its innards spilling out over an old copy of the *Press and Journal*. Offshore Dave is sipping something from my mother's *Wallace and Gromit* mug. Judging by the hip flask beside his elbow, it's not just coffee. His boots have left gouts of muck beneath the table and no one has bothered to pick up the broken china.

We venture in. I fill the kettle; River sits down and takes off his boots. Eventually, Dad glances up, screwdriver posed as delicately as a chopstick.

'Where have you been?'

Is it a trick question? Does he know? Maybe Piotr didn't manage to disable the software in time. The thought of him observing our frantic drive to the caravan makes me feel sick. When neither of us replies, he tries a different tack.

'When were you going to tell me?'

River and I glance at each other. My mouth goes dry, making it difficult to speak.

'Tell you what?'

He places the screwdriver down on the paper. His hands are obscured slightly by the radio case, but I can see he's sorting through the bits – the springs and screws, tubes and wires. It looks like he's assembling a homemade bomb.

'When I started to clean this up, I was puzzled by a black component peeking over this transformer on the left. In the scheme of things, it didn't seem to fit.' He scratches his beard. 'It puzzled me. When I turned the set over and traced the wiring, I discovered it was the power supply rectifier!'

He grins at Dave, who grins back, even though he hasn't a clue what a rectifier is.

'Rectifiers of this vintage are often unreliable, so . . .' Dad sorts through some more parts. 'I've decided to replace it with a modern silicon diode. Ah – here's what I'm looking for!'

With a flourish, he produces a black feather. Pinched between finger and thumb, he holds it up to the light. I'm transfixed by its blue-black glint. River tries to catch my eye, but I can't look away.

'Just get to the point,' I whisper.

'The point being,' he says, 'a little detective work and attention to detail sheds light on most things.'

I can hear the ticking of the clock; Dave slurping his coffee. My insides have turned to slush.

'Shelby Smith appears to have acquired feathers in his cap that he never had before.' He peers closely at the object in his fingers. 'Crow feathers, to be exact. Now, I can't imagine Shelby Smith making an Easter bonnet out of that tatty old fedora, can you, Offshore?'

Dave shakes his head and chortles through closed lips. Dad smiles slowly.

'So, naturally, I'm wondering who did this. Who might put a feather or two in his cap?'

I bite my lip. I'm a rabbit with a hawk circling above. 'That doesn't mean anything.'

'No. But this does.' With a magical flourish, Dad produces Mum's scarf. The red one with the owls on it. 'Lying on the seat in his caravan.'

33

They say time stands still when you've had a shock, but I can still hear that damn clock ticking. Dave's smirk hovers above the mug; the feather rotates through 360 degrees and flutters to the ground as Dad gets to his feet. He picks up the radio and hurls it across the room. River dives out of the way, and the sound of the crash makes every nerve in my body shrink.

'When were you going to tell me she's alive? It was all a scam, wasn't it? She faked it.'

'We didn't know.' River straightens cautiously.

'We hadn't a clue until today.' My eyelid twitches. The sudden silence is deafening.

My father stalks towards us, winding the red scarf around the knuckles of his right hand, like a boxer. I shrink away from him. He shoves his face into mine and I can see the spittle glistening on his beard.

'I'm not stupid. I know you've been twisting the knife. She was perfectly fine until you started talking about Citizens fucking Advice and Women's Aid and all the other nonsense.'

I narrow my eyes at him. Now is not the time to accuse him of cloning her phone. I need to keep it together.

'I don't know what you're talking about.'

'Bullshit. You couldn't just leave her alone. Even from a distance you were winding her up, pulling her strings—'

'*Me* pulling her strings? You're the bloody control freak!'

'Everything I've done, I've done for this family. Just trying to keep the family afloat, but I can see now the ship was full of rats! I knew she was carrying on with someone, but I didn't know who. Not until Shelby Smith did a moonlight flit and it all clicked into place.' He taps his temple. 'I took him in. Looked out for him like . . . like *family*, and this is how they both repay me! Well, I've given him a little warning and she'll get a taste of the same. I take it she's still up there, on the hills? Channelling fucking Finella? We all know what happened to her.'

I open my mouth to protest, to speak up for Finella, for my mother, but it's pointless. He's already reaching for his car keys.

'We didn't see her. We did go up there, but she wasn't there.' I blurt the words out, not knowing if I'm making things better or worse.

'Dave, we'll take the dogs. Give them the scent.' He hands over the scarf.

'It's dark!' I protest. 'What's the point?'

My father looks at me with cold eyes. 'The point is she'll be all tucked up for the night. Her tent is missing from the garage – I checked.' He jerks his head at River. 'Come on. Wherever she's holed up, she'll come out for you.'

River glances at me. I incline my head a fraction and pretend to study the floor tiles as the three of them troop out. The slam of the door shudders through me. The van rumbles past the window, then there's a pause as someone gets out to open the gate. I strain to follow its progress along the drive, imagining Sharon Duthie peering out of her bathroom window, wondering what the hell is going on. I wait a second or two before coming to life and sprinting to the door.

I'd taken the precaution of locking the car, and I'd even kept the keys hidden in my jeans pocket, instead of throwing them down beside the kettle like we normally do. My hands are trembling so much that I press the wrong button on the fob and nothing happens. I pull up inches from the car and I press again. The lights flash, but still nothing. Starting to panic, I jab randomly at the fob until I hear the clunk of the locks.

I'm transported back to that other time, that other car. I feel as though I'm moving through treacle as I depress the catch on the boot and lift the lid.

In the cramped space, my mother stirs. She's been lying in the foetal position, eyes scrunched tightly shut. Drinking in the sudden rush of fresh air, she reaches out to me. Her hands are bone white and curled into claws, and a moment of sheer revulsion grips me. I am my father, putting her through this. Dehumanising her.

'I'm so sorry. If there'd been any other way . . . Here, let me help you.'

She struggles upright. Her lips are dry, and she licks them but doesn't speak. I'd persuaded her into the boot a few miles down the road. 'It's the only way,' I'd told her. 'Think of the Trojan Horse! You're Helen of Troy!' I'd wiped a tear from her grubby cheek and shut her in the dark. It wasn't Helen of Troy who was inside the horse, River had reminded me, when I jumped back into the driver's seat. It was a whole bunch of Greek warriors, slipping into the enemy camp by stealth, under the very noses of the enemy. 'Exactly,' I'd replied. Then he said that Helen of Troy was the one who caused it all. We travelled in silence after that.

Now, I gently grab my mother's arm and pull her into a sitting position.

'You're better than Helen of Troy. You're a strong, clever warrior. You're Finella.'

She scrambles out, and I hold her for a second. She feels cold and a bit wobbly. Both of us, I know, are envisaging that other time, over ten years ago, when I helped her out of a boot in a blood-red garage. That time, she'd limped into her own home with one shoe missing, smelling of mildew and mice.

'Oh, Mum . . .' I'm no longer sure which of us is trembling, but we cling together, making a stronger whole.

'*You* are Finella. Finella Rook,' she says. 'You have to make this stop.'

It's what I've always been afraid of.

She stands in the middle of the kitchen and blinks. I suppose she never expected to be back here so soon. Or ever. That wasn't part of the plan. Her attention wanders to the shards of crockery on the floor. She stoops to pick up a rose-patterned sliver.

'Grandma Rook's china?' She widens her eyes at me. 'Did he do this?'

I shake my head. 'That was me.'

She turns the fragment over in her hand, as if she's hunting for clues.

In a bid to take control of a very weird situation, I go into full hospitality mode, clapping my hands together briskly. 'Right. Let's get you sorted. It'll be a bit of a squeeze and you'll have to be very quiet, but—'

'What? What the hell are we doing here?' She drops the fragment of china into the pedal bin and wipes her hand on a tea towel, as if it has somehow contaminated her. 'You said I'd be safe. This doesn't feel like safe to me.'

I catch her hand in mine. 'Believe me, this is the safest place. I'm keeping you in my bedroom. He never goes in there. It's the one place he would never look.' Her eyes flicker with doubt, and I plunge on. 'And we've done it! We've Trojan-horsed his ass while he's running around the country looking for . . . you.'

The *you* strikes a wrong note. She drops my hand and turns to confront me.

'He knows? He knows I'm still alive?'

Shit. I scrape my fingers through my hair. 'It wasn't our fault! He spotted the crow feathers in Shelby's hat and put two and two together, and then he found your scarf, the one you were wearing when you . . . fell. That confirmed it.'

'Shelby's hat? Does that mean he knows . . . me and Shelby?'

I nod.

She's staring at me like I've suddenly sprouted snakes where my hair should be. I lift my hands, but she bats me away when

I try to touch her again. Her eyes have gone all faraway. 'So that's why we couldn't find my scarf when we were gathering up my stuff.'

We'd shoved her tent and the few things she had with her into the boot too, and covered them with an old bit of carpet. I hadn't paid too much attention to the missing scarf. Maybe I should have.

'He was a bit angry.' I bite my lip in the sort of coy gesture I might have used as a teenager, but it isn't going to get me out of trouble this time. Mum raises an eyebrow at my under-statement. 'They've gone to search the woods.'

'Who?'

'Dad and Offshore and River. River will keep them off the scent.'

'In the dark?'

I don't repeat Dad's words, but she knows his MO by now.

'Oh Christ.' She sinks down onto a chair. 'I need to find out about Shel. You should have seen what they did—' Her voice cracks, but I don't go near her again. I'm not sure I know how to cope with this. I've always wondered what I'd do if I came across the scene of a traffic accident – would I panic or step up to the plate? It looks like I'm about to find out how far I can go.

34

I've avoided my parents' bedroom since she left. Overnight, it had become grey and severe, with the curtains half drawn and all evidence of Mum banished behind the wardrobe doors. Now I'm forced to commit a daring raid on enemy territory in order to collect fresh clothes. Behind the bathroom door, the shower is going at full pelt, and the landing is filling up with the scent of jasmine and cloves. I sent Mum in there with an armful of the fancy products she's always been scared to use, but perhaps that was a mistake. I wonder if I'll be able to get rid of the telltale scent before my father gets home.

In my parents' room, the double bed is neatly made, pillows plumped, a strip of blue-striped pyjama visible between pillow and duvet. It looks oddly vulnerable. I wonder if he misses her, whether all his bluster and spite is just a cover for a broken heart.

Stop right there. That's the very thought pattern that kept her here, wasting the best years of her life with a man who didn't know how to love her. All the excuses she made for him – *he's tired, he's working too hard, he had a difficult childhood* – all covering up the truth. My father is a cold, cruel man who will never change.

I rummage through cupboards and drawers, grabbing underwear, tops, a fresh pair of jeans, a hairbrush; hastily rearranging the remaining clothes so Dad won't get suspicious. We're good at that – rearranging things so we don't cause a wrinkle in his day. Just as I'm about to close the last drawer, I discover a couple of leaflets, carefully hidden under an old bathing suit. (When was the last time my mother went swimming?) I pull them out with difficulty, my arms full of clothes, and shove the drawer closed with my knee.

I'd been on a night out in Hanoi when I got that tearful phone call from my mother, the one that made me face up to what was really going on here. I couldn't get any sense out of her at first, and I was a bit drunk, which didn't help, but eventually it sank in. *I can't do this any more. I need help.* I'm not sure what the catalyst was, or why she suddenly cracked, but I spent the next few hours on the phone to various agencies in the UK. I badly wanted to scoop her up and get her out of there, but I couldn't get the time off work, and all the earnest people I spoke to at a distance said the same thing: she has to be the one to seek help. You can't do it for her.

So I texted her all the information I could get. All the phone numbers that could have been her salvation: Women's Aid, the National Domestic Violence Helpline, Victim Support. Even the police, which was a non-starter, given our family policy. Maybe she would have gone down that path, if he hadn't been receiving all her personal messages on his cloned phone. I'm not sure I want to know how that conversation went, but whatever happened, she decided to take matters into her own hands.

We meet on the landing. She emerges from the bathroom in my fluffy robe with her hair turbaned into a white towel, smiling her gap-tooth smile and looking relaxed, more like herself. If things weren't so crazy and dangerous, this might be a normal mother-daughter night. We should be bingeing on a box set and eating Pringles, not cowering upstairs, waiting for the slam of the door.

I hustle her into my room. 'Here are some of your clothes.'

'You didn't make it obvious?'

'No. I used to live here, remember? I'm going to make you something to eat, and then I'll try and ring the hospital again. I'll say I'm his . . . Oh my God.' A thought strikes me, something so huge I can barely put it into words. 'I can say I'm his daughter . . .'

Mum's face crumples and she flops down on the edge of my bed. 'You're not,' she says bluntly. 'Many's the time I've wished you were. It might have spurred me on to leave, to get out of here. If he gets better – *when* he gets better – we need to get away. That was the plan, to go down south. I don't know where. Now that your dad knows I faked it all . . .'

She gives a hopeless little shrug. I thrust her clothes onto a chair with such force that the pile starts to collapse. 'One step at a time. You should think about that refuge in Aberdeen I told you about.' I brandish the leaflets. 'Remember I sent you these? You'd be safe there. They have security on the doors and everything.'

She shivers. 'I couldn't bear that. It would be like being in jail. And anyway, what about Shelby? If Shel's not dead already, your father will finish him off to get at me.'

There's no denying it. I sigh and sit down on the bed too. Both of us stare at the floral carpet for a long time.

'Plan A definitely hasn't worked,' she whispers eventually. 'We need a Plan B.'

The pattern on the carpet seems to shift. My eyes follow the creeping leaf design into ever-decreasing spirals. Even though I don't want to know the answer, I ask the question.

'Like what?'

'Plan B is . . . You have to kill your father.'

35

I'm in the kitchen when my father comes back. My brain is running on so many tracks it feels like St Pancras in there. I'm replaying my mother's preposterous plan, which goes against all the tenets of motherhood.

You have to kill your father.

When she said those words, every bit of heat in me had trickled away. I told her the idea was ridiculous, that it made no sense, but she gripped my arm, nails as sharp as bird claws. It has to be me. It'd be easy for me to escape, she said, to go back to the life I had before. She's supposed to be dead – and besides, she couldn't bear to be locked up. Her place is with Shelby now. He's all she's ever wanted.

She was babbling, speaking half to herself, and all I could do was stare at her and wonder – yet again – how we got into this mess.

She wants the king executed, but she wants me to go down for it.

And then there are the details of the phone conversation I've just had with the hospital in Aberdeen, plus all the little anxieties – the fragrant fug in the bathroom, the rifled drawers. Will my father rumble us? Can I pull this off?

Then I realise I'm making scrambled eggs and toast for two and quickly chuck a couple of rounds in the bin. And two cups of tea! I fire one of them into the sink just as Dad opens the door. They all stroll in – Dad, Dave and River, with the two dogs – bringing with them the scent of the night: dank vegetation and foxes. That's probably from the dogs. Their tongues are lolling like they've been chasing something.

Dad pulls out his chair. He looks suspiciously calm, but that means nothing. He is a volcano waiting to blow. I try to catch River's attention, but he has perfected his poker face and gives nothing away. The earlier injury to his lip is beginning to dry up, but there's a fresh scratch on his cheek, as if he's been attacked by trees.

'The bird has flown.' Offshore Dave sidles up too close to me as I refill the kettle. I shy away from the smell of sweat and fuel. I want to say my mother isn't a bird – or if she is, she's a crow who'll peck your fucking eyes out – but I keep quiet. When Dave fails to get a reaction, he takes himself off to the table.

Dad rubs his beard. 'What I don't understand about you two' – his stony gaze flicks between my brother and me – 'is this. If you only just found out your mother was alive, wouldn't you try and bring her back here?'

Neither of us speak. I glance at River, but he is leaning against the counter, staring at his feet.

'Out of loyalty to me, even?' our father continues. 'Look what she's put me through!' His voice is gathering strength, volume. 'I thought she was dead. *You two* should have brought her back to me. Her place is HERE!'

He stands up so suddenly that his chair rocks backwards. One of the dogs whines. This time, River does catch my eye. Every sinew in my body is tight, as if I'm preparing to run. My father's voice rattles my ears.

'Have I taught you NOTHING about family loyalty? We Rooks stay together, no matter what. It was your duty to bring her home.'

I'm so scared my insides have turned to water, and my gaze is fixed on the floor. One of the dogs pauses by my elbow and sniffs. I stiffen. A wet nose travels down my thigh, snuffles at the back of my knee. I hear a growl starting low in its throat. It must be scenting my mother. I hold my breath. River opens the biscuit tin and makes a big play of breaking a digestive in two. Both dogs are immediately distracted and sit to attention, drooling. I start to breathe.

'So.' Dad sits down at the table again. He steeples his fingers and glares over the top of them. 'Your mother can't have gone far, unless you helped her escape.'

'No,' River says, too quickly. He glances at me.

'She can't have gone far,' Dave echoes. 'She's got no car. Dogs got the scent up there all right, but—'

'Maybe she got the bus.' All eyes swing to me. I'm aware I'm gabbling, but anything to keep them away from her. 'I . . . I called the hospital. Shelby's there, so – so maybe she got the bus to Aberdeen. She'd want to see how Shelby's doing.'

Dad looks at me with a strange light in his eyes.

'Oh yes. She'd want to see how Shelby's doing. That's the answer. You didn't think of that, did you, Dave?'

They grin at each other, but Dad's expression makes my blood run cold. I have one more card to play. As I place the mugs carefully on the table, I slip a glossy leaflet down beside the milk jug, where, until recently, PC Sampson's pastel bereavement literature had sat. I can't get my head around the journey we're on. It's making me dizzy.

Dad is quizzing Dave about bus timetables. Now he spots the leaflet and picks it up. I watch his face harden as he reads it.

'A women's refuge?' He glances up at me. 'What the fuck? You've been filling her head with more of this nonsense, haven't you?'

My mouth makes a downward turn. 'Nothing to do with me. I expect she contacted them a while ago.'

He holds up the leaflet and gives it a stinging slap with the back of his fingers. 'Because she had such a rotten life with me, didn't she, Dave?'

Dave chuckles. 'Rotten, boss. Didn't know she was born, more like. All this . . .' He gazes around the kitchen in wonder.

'Well, I think we'll pay Aberdeen a little visit tomorrow.

The hospital first, see if she's sitting by his bedside, and if not' – he waves the leaflet – 'we know where she'll be.'

I catch River's eye. According to the woman I've just spoken to on the phone, an unidentified male had been admitted and a detective is waiting to interview him. Now, despite everything I've ever been taught, I'm hoping against hope that the police can protect Shelby.

My mother is dozing fitfully in the centre of my double bed when I finally escape upstairs. Sighing, I sit down at the dressing table and scowl into the mirror. My healthy tan has faded into dull exhaustion. My mind continues to perform cartwheels, but I cannot see an easy way out of this mess. Mum's Plan B comes back to haunt me, and I dare to imagine a scenario where we are left in peace to live as we wish. The reality is that she's hurt my father's pride, sidestepped his authority. If it becomes known that she faked her death to get away from him, it will be the ultimate humiliation. Rooks are not allowed to break rank – even my gap year was pushing it – and he won't rest until he's brought her back into the fold. Would he kill her, like she seems to think? I've read those leaflets. On average, two women a week are killed by a partner or ex-partner in this country. I look across at my mother's face. The deep frown line is still visible between her closed eyes and her lashes are flickering. Am I going to let her become a statistic?

A light knocking makes me leap up. The door opens, but it's only River. I press a finger to my lips, and he glances at the bed and nods.

'Why didn't you tell me you'd phoned the hospital?' he whispers.

'I couldn't. I didn't get a chance. And anyway, I don't have much information. They wouldn't tell me anything over the phone.'

'Just as well I'm on the case, then.' I realise he's smiling. 'Shelby called me just now.'

'What? Where is he? How is he?'

'He's discharged himself from hospital. Just walked out!'

'Oh, thank God.' The relief is overwhelming. 'Typical Shelby. Is he okay? At least he won't be there when they go to the hospital tomorrow.'

'That's why he left. He said Dad won't give up until someone dies.' We both shudder. 'Anyway, he says he's going to lay low for a while. He has a mate in Aberdeen. He's okay – busted ribs, concussion – but he says he'll live to fight another day.'

We both look at Mum. His choice of words feels chillingly prophetic.

36

Fifteen Days After

The next day, Dad leaves early, taking River with him. He doesn't say where he's going, but he's taken the leaflet too. I hope to goodness Shelby is lying low. Offshore Dave is left in charge, although we all know it's Julie who'll keep everything going. I can see her through the windows of the Portacabin, fielding phone calls while Dave slopes off to smoke behind the toilets. I don't want to go near her. I can't deal with her sympathy while I'm harbouring a dead woman in my room.

Even with Dad away, I daren't let Mum downstairs. She's restless – talking about crows and the woods and the garden – but leaving the fragile safety of that room is not an option. All we need is for Sharon Duthie to catch the vaguest glimpse of her and the news of the resurrection will spread around the countryside like wildfire.

I bring her a cup of tea and some toast after Dad leaves. 'I'm worried about River. He's being torn in two.'

She's brushing her hair at the dressing table, sitting where I'd sat and worried the night before. The resemblance between us is clear, although I see my brother there too – the unruly hair, the half-shy, half-defiant expression.

'That last day, down by the waterfall, we talked more than we'd ever talked before,' she said. 'I never let on to him about Shelby and me, but I told him I had to disappear. It was the only way I could get away from Lawler. He argued with me. He said I'd be abandoning him.'

'It's true. You really think Dad's a good role model?'

'Do you really think he'd let me walk out of here with his son?'

She has me there. River is Dad's shadow. He has a much better relationship with him than I've ever had, though he can see his flaws too.

'I told River we could meet up at some point, that I wasn't going to be out of his life – or yours – for good, but I needed a . . . a breathing space. He said he understood.'

'No wonder he's so bloody angry. He's trying to please everyone. He's a teenager, and you've put all this' – I wave my hand distractedly – 'all this responsibility on him. Imagine what it was like for him, having to come home and lie for all he was worth. Lying to his dad, for God's sake.'

In the mirror, I see tears forming in her eyes.

'He was so full of rage,' she whispers. I think of Mandy Cotton and family services. 'I didn't know how to handle him. I was scared he was turning into his father, and I could see everything getting worse. So much worse.'

'I think there might be more to this.' I rest my hand on her shoulder. 'He seems to spend a lot of time with Ned.'

'Ned's a friend. A kind, compassionate friend. Someone who's not covered in filth and constantly cursing. And River is only fifteen, for goodness' sake.'

'I'm not saying there's anything going on, but River's at that age where he's getting to know about himself. His preferences. Who's going to be there for him when he's feeling his way through the next few years?'

She bites her lip. A wave of anger quivers through me. It's going to be me, isn't it? If I want to be there for my brother, I'm going to have to give up my wandering lifestyle. I'm going to have to move back home and be the mediator, the buffer, just as my mother was. Meanwhile, Mum will be travelling the roads with the love of her life. It will be the making of her. The irony of this role reversal isn't lost on me – nor, probably, on her. When I glance back at the mirror, her eyes are watchful, calculating.

'So let's talk about Plan B,' she says.

37

The longer Dad and River are gone, the more agitated I become. It's impossible to settle, and I find myself trying to second-guess their progress, where they might be and what they are getting up to. My thoughts keep straying to Shelby too. Is he okay? What if he's taken a turn for the worse and is readmitted to the ward? I torment myself with bleak scenarios: Shelby lying collapsed in the hospital grounds; or Dad looming over his bed with a pillow, and River unable to prevent murder. I don't even want to be around Mum just now. Her presence reminds me of how close we are sailing to the wind. I have no idea what's going to happen next.

I'm outside, mooching around the cars, when a familiar voice stops me in my tracks.

'Hi, Ellie.'

Piotr catches me off guard, and I have no time to temper my reaction. Blood rushes to my face and I stutter a greeting. I'm shocked at how pleased I am to see him. It's only natural, I tell myself, after all that's been going on, to crave a friendly face. He's like one of those bothies on the beach – a port in a storm. It doesn't mean there's anything deeper.

'I thought you were gone – going – catching a bus?'

'I had to stick around.'

Warmth blossoms deep inside me, and something unfamiliar. Hope. A fragile, beating butterfly wing. With a rush, I realise I want to confide in him. Share the awful burden that my mother is alive and well and living in bedroomsville, and I don't know what to do. I want him to see that I'm out of my depth and throw me a lifeline. But I don't. Even though we've seen each other naked, trust is too intimate.

Julie is at the Portacabin window, sorting through pink invoices. I don't realise I'm staring at her until she glances up, the way people sometimes do when they can feel your gaze upon them. I imagine her weighing things up, speculating about why I'm having an intimate conversation with Piotr. Do we look intimate? I step away from him.

'Thanks, Piotr. I really appreciate it.'

'Um, Ellie – I *had* to stay. I have . . . an appointment. I cannot leave town just yet.'

'Oh.' The butterfly wing stops beating. I try to read his face. There's a little nerve twitching near his mouth, and it puts a hitch in my breathing. Doctor's appointment? Is he ill? Or have the council caught up with him for trying to make a home out of a condemned building? I wait for him to elaborate, but he closes up. I'm so familiar with that feeling.

'I will do my morning shift first.' He glances at the yard without enthusiasm. 'But—'

I want to reach out to him, but Julie is still watching with greedy interest.

'I'm glad I have seen you.'

'I don't want you to think bad of me.'

'You mean about the tracking and stuff? That was coercion.'

He wrinkles his brow. 'Coer-shun?'

'It's a word for what my father does. Forget it.'

'I will not forget. I will not forget you.'

This time, I do touch him. I run my fingers over his forearm, and the blond hairs bristle beneath my touch. It's not enough, but enough for now. I'm not sure what he's getting at, and Offshore Dave is watching us, slouching against the Portacabin with an unpleasant grin on his dirty face. What is this? First Julie and now Dave.

Pity none of the staff ever noticed what was going on under their noses before it got to the point of no return.

After Piotr leaves, I sit out in the front garden for as long as I can. The patchwork cushion is still mouldering away on the bench where my mother left it, the day before she disappeared. It seems an apt metaphor for how things have turned out. Something is rotten in this little kingdom. I listen to the sharp mew of the gulls, the faraway shush of the sea, all the while straining to hear the distant sound of a car engine that will herald the return of the men.

I'm still trying to come to terms with my mother loving someone who isn't my father. In some ways, the fact that it's Shelby makes it worse. I'm already mourning the easy, comfortable relationship I used to enjoy with him. Now he feels like a stranger, and I'm being forced to think about my mother's personal life – her *sex* life Where did they do it behind my father's back? In the caravan? In the woods? I don't want to contemplate it, but I can understand my father's jealousy. It's enough to drive anyone insane.

A horrible image floats into my head, of me pinning the teenage Katie Coutts to the changing-room floor because she dared to make a move on my boyfriend. I can hardly bear to think about it, and now my mother is suggesting something far more evil. Plan B – the cold-blooded, premeditated murder of my own father. It's a world away from simply lashing out in anger. My mother is turning into a liability. Will I be able to steer her away from her scheming or, like everything else, is it going to be taken out of my hands?

I'm afraid of losing control of the situation. I'm being blown off course by an unrelenting wind and I'm afraid of what I might do. Self-pitying tears smudge my cheeks. *What if?*

What if?

I am my father's daughter. I'm backed into a corner, if the white mist rises and I'm pushed . . . who knows what I'd be capable of?

A thin plume of smoke is rising from the Duthies' chimney. I imagine them going about their ordinary little lives – Sharon reading *Woman's Weekly* with the radio on; Liam looking for jobs on Gumtree. At least he was able to boomerang back to a messy, chaotic, normal mother, whereas I've been plunged into a nightmare. Hot shame fills me. My mother is a victim. We're all victims and it's making us crazy.

A subtle smoker's cough from across the road grabs my attention. I walk to the garden gate and there's Liam, having a fly puff in his front garden. He raises his hand and wanders over.

'Hey. How are things?'

Oddly, I do not feel the need to blurt things out to Liam. My family affairs slink away under a rock and wait.

'Och, you know. Getting by.'

He takes a drag of his cigarette. 'Saw your dad going out earlier. And River.'

'They were going to look at a car.'

'Oh.' He nods, and we lapse into silence. 'Saw Rocky too, a while back. On his bike. Pedalling like fuck!' He laughs at his own wit. 'Maybe he had an appointment.'

His choice of word makes my skin prickle. 'Why would you say that?'

He raises his shoulders and lets them drop. 'Just something I heard.'

'What? What did you hear?'

He holds up a hand. 'I don't want to make things worse for you.' His eyes, glittering with untold secrets, tell a different story.

'Believe me, things cannot get any worse.'

'Well, they're saying that . . . that Rocky had a hand in your mum's death. It stands to reason – we don't know anything about him, his background or anything. He could have a criminal record. He could have done this sort of thing before.'

Cold is creeping up my spine. 'What sort of thing?'

'Befriending a woman, and then when the going gets tough—'

I make an impatient noise. 'Wait a minute – who's saying this? Who's making up this nonsense?'

His little-boy face takes on a certain smugness, like he's stolen all the apples. 'People have conversations in pubs, and sometimes they reach the right ears.'

'Police ears? You had a conversation in the pub with an off-duty cop, is that what you're saying?'

His expression crumples. 'No! It wasn't me!'

'Oh yes, I can see it now. You and Danny Findlater having a pint. He's a DI now, isn't he?'

He nods before he can stop himself. 'It's only what everyone else was thinking. And anyway, they can't arrest him – not until more evidence comes to light. They've asked him to come in voluntarily, because he was off work sick the day she fell – if she fell – and he has no alibi.'

'But Liam, River was there, when Mum . . . when she fell. If Piotr was involved, he would have seen him. You've concocted a story, haven't you? You've grassed him up.'

I keep my voice low, even though I want to snarl at him. What the hell am I going to do now? How the hell can I let Piotr take the rap for something that never happened? Especially when the very subject of the missing persons inquiry is upstairs, sitting at my dressing table?

Liam drops the fag end onto the road and presses a hand against his chest. 'So I get the blame for doing the right thing? I might've known you'd be on his side.'

'There are no sides.'

'Oh, I think there are.'

I stare at him. 'You're jealous? You think I'm shagging Piotr, so you thought you'd get your own back by peddling lies about him?' I make a noise like a moan. 'What have you done? I really, really don't need this right now. There is nothing to be jealous about, because there is nothing – you and me' – I wave my hand back and forth between us – 'NOTHING.'

'Fuck off.' Liam makes an angry gesture with his hand and goes to storm off, but then he bounces back. His face is pale and hard. 'Fuck right off. If you don't want me, fine, but I'm sure as hell not letting you end up with some foreigner!'

I gasp. My father's words roll back through the tears. *Get off my property.*

'I belong to no one,' I say through gritted teeth. 'I'm my own person.'

It's time I took control.

38

Back in the house, I hunt for the very thing I discarded just two weeks ago. I was too sure of my ground back then, still sticking to the old patterns. No outside interference. Keep it in the family. But now all I can think of is Piotr, who doesn't deserve to be caught up in this mess.

The table is littered with debris that no one has any intention of clearing. I suppose I'll have to do it eventually, but right now I have bigger things on my mind. I move the stone-cold teapot and the milk jug. There's no sign of the pastel leaflets – I remember dumping them in the bin – but there's nothing else there either. I go to the 'junk drawer' and rifle through the old phone chargers and batteries. And there I find what I'm looking for: PC Lorraine Sampson's business card.

Lorraine crosses her legs neatly and sits back with an air of expectation. Across the table, I fidget in my father's seat and wonder where the hell to start. I feel like my rap sheet is written on my face in large print: lying about my mother's disappearance; wasting police time; concealing a felony (and a felon); covering up a serious assault; and probably aiding and abetting a truant. I don't have time to dwell on it though. Dad will be back soon and I can't bear to think about what he'll say – what he'll do – if he finds a cop in his kitchen. Steeling myself, I take a deep breath, clasping my hands together like I'm praying.

'I think you've taken Piotr in for questioning, and you need to let him go. He didn't do anything. I know he didn't.'

PC Sampson hitches up a little in her seat. 'Piotr?'

'Polish guy. Works here. Sorry, I don't even know his surname.'
I cringe inside.

She pauses for a beat; glances at her notebook. 'Ah yes. We've had some new intelligence to suggest that he was quite close with your mother, so he attended for interview voluntarily this afternoon.'

'And? Being friendly with people doesn't point to anything. My mother was friendly with lots of people.'

That isn't strictly true, but this whole thing is ridiculous. Surely PC Sampson can see that?

'Ellie, you called me because you said you had some new information about your mother.' She puts down her notebook and mirrors my position, leaning on the table. We must look very earnest. A sly glance at the notebook reveals only a few squiggles on an otherwise blank page. All apparently low-key, but my heart is pounding with such force I feel sick.

'Yes, my mother. You see . . . it's complicated.'

'Mmm.'

'The thing is . . .' I avoid her eyes and focus on my fingers, picking at the last stubborn remnants of Beach Gold. 'My mother had a reason to disappear.'

I can sense Lorraine's sudden tension. I can see tomorrow's headlines in the *Gazette*: LOCAL MOTHER ENDURES YEARS OF HELL. I'm betraying my mother, my family. All our dysfunctional bits are going to be on display like animal parts in a butcher's window.

'She suffered years of emotional and physical abuse at the hands of my father. My brother and me, we witnessed it all, but she never spoke up and we didn't either.' I swallow, and it sounds loud, even to me. Lorraine leans in closer. There's a softening about her eyes.

'It's okay, Ellie. Go on.'

'We've never been a family for letting folk in, and I guess I thought we just had to live with it, until she phoned me one day, saying that she just wanted to disappear. She had it all planned.

I tried to get her help, I really did, but she thought . . . she thought this was her only option.'

'Did she fear for her life, Ellie?'

I hesitate. She isn't writing this down, and she seems to sense my hesitation. 'This is just between us at this stage. It's all right – just tell me the truth in your own words.'

'Yes. She thought my father would kill her.' Best not to complicate things with Shelby.

'Is that how it seemed to you?'

I nod wordlessly. Have I signed the king's death warrant? We sit in silence for a beat or two, as Lorraine deliberates on her choice of words. 'So, just to be clear, your mother faked her death and you and your brother have been covering it up? And your brother is fifteen, sixteen?'

'Not quite sixteen.'

'Mmm. And where is your mother now, Ellie?'

My eyes stray to the ceiling. Slowly, understanding dawns on her face, and she indicates upwards. 'You hid her in the house? In the attic?'

'In my bedroom.'

A ghost of a smile. 'That's . . . novel. You didn't think your father would look there?'

'Not in my bedroom, no.'

'Does she know you've contacted me?'

'No.'

'I'm sure she's very afraid, but the thing is, she *must* disclose the abuse herself, in order for me to get her the appropriate help. Do you understand? Faking your own death isn't a crime, provided there are no financial or criminal factors involved.'

'It isn't?' I grasp this fragile flicker of hope. 'She was driven to it. My father, he once locked her in the boot of a car, and some nights she used to sleep in my bed to get away from him. I don't know what went on, but I remember once he came in and dragged her out of bed by the hair. I was only about ten or eleven, and I tried to hang on to her. We were both crying but he was stronger. She told me to stay in my room. My whole childhood was about closed doors and raised voices and . . . the aftermath. I suppose I only ever saw the aftermath. My mother's white face and red eyes. And my father – always so bloody normal, like nothing could touch him.'

I press my hands to the panicky rise and fall of my belly. I'm breathless. I don't think I've ever uttered such a monologue in my entire life. I feel light and shaky, like a breath of wind will send me floating to the ceiling.

Lorraine sighs, as if her life is full of such incidents, and I suppose it is. 'That's the real issue here, Ellie. Domestic abuse is a criminal offence. If your mother wishes to press charges, we can make this stop.'

Behind me, the hall door creaks, and I spin around. Mum's standing there. I don't know how long she's been out in the hall listening, but she doesn't seem surprised to find me deep in conversation with a cop. She is blank-faced and silent.

Lorraine rises from her seat. 'Imelda, Ellie's been very brave and told me about what's been happening, but I'd like to hear it from you. Maybe you could pop the kettle on, Ellie?'

I jump up, glad to have someone else taking charge. For the first time since Shelby held me to his heart, I feel safe. I could have reached out like this at any time, and we would have been rescued. So much wasted time. Tears prickle my eyes. PC Sampson, with her leaflets and her razor-sharp grasp of the situation, is going to find a way through this. I go about the whole tea-making business with one eye on my mother's face. She doesn't look like someone who intends on sitting down and drinking with the enemy, and I realise with cold dread that she's wearing her coat and boots.

'I'm sorry for wasting your time,' Mum says eventually. 'I was having a bad day and I just wanted to disappear. I'm sure you've felt the same. You just want to leave the world behind for a short while.'

I drop the teabags and turn to face her. Lorraine is standing with her back to me and I can't see her expression, but her blonde ponytail is nodding subtly, even though I'm sure she's never experienced anything of the kind.

'Mum . . .' I'm just about to plead, to coax the right words out of her, when the back door flies open, admitting a shaft of cold air and the shuffling of work boots. After all my listening for the king's return, I missed it.

My father assesses the scene as River closes the door. A frozen tableau of women: his missing wife, a police officer and the daughter he doesn't trust.

Boom.

He sums up the situation in an instant and surges forward to take my mother in his arms. I swear he's weeping into her neck, but all I can see are her huge, stricken eyes. A deer awaiting the final bullet. I pray that Lorraine sees it too.

He holds her away from him, gazing down into her unresponsive face. 'Imelda, my love. We've been so worried about you. Me, Ellie, River – we were beside ourselves. Whatever's gone wrong, whatever made you do this, we can work it out.'

I'm speechless, and again Lorraine takes charge. 'Imelda, would you like to speak to me in private?'

Dad turns to Lorraine, an arm about his wife's shoulders. 'No need. She's home, thank God. I think it's fair to say her mental health hasn't been the best of late, eh, Imelda? That old black dog.' He makes a sympathetic face and my mother nods. She actually nods.

'Depression,' she agrees. 'I've suffered for years. I'm so sorry for all the trouble I've caused.'

Dad gives her a hearty squeeze, and as Lorraine goes to speak, he launches into full hospitality mode, silencing her with his bonhomie. 'Ellie, tea and sandwiches, there's a good girl. How about we chat over a nice spot of lunch, PC Sampson? River, open a tin of salmon. I know we face this whole issue of wasting police time, and I fully intend to make reparation for that . . .'

There's a note of panic in his camaraderie, and as he waffles on, I catch my mother's eye. How could she not speak up for herself when she had the chance? How can she let him put such a spin on things? It feels like a betrayal. Her face gives nothing away, and all my hopes of rescue begin to recede. I'm drowning in fear.

I seem to be watching everything from a distance. PC Sampson is collecting her things together, preparing to leave, as my father smooths her way with false words. She doesn't look happy about it, and inwardly I'm pleading with her to stay. *Don't leave us.* The power has shifted back to Mum, but she's scared to use it, and without her cooperation, we're all in limbo.

There are goodbyes: Dad, pumping the police officer's hand as if it's the most normal thing in the world; my mother's cracked whisper; Lorraine's strained 'I'll be in touch'. I get myself to the door first and manage to catch her eye on the way out, willing her to read my distress signals.

Outside, the yard is deserted, the grabber standing idle. Everyone's gone home, although I wasn't aware of them leaving. No white van, no lilac Mini, just PC Sampson's squad car and Dad's Range Rover, parked arrogantly across three spaces.

And hitched to the back of it – Shelby's caravan.

I go weak. I stare at it, searching the battered exterior for hidden meaning. Shelby's caravan, spattered with mud from the road, ferns trailing from the tow bar. Lorraine has clocked it too, but she has no point of reference. My father is a scrap dealer. She has no way of knowing whether this is out of the ordinary. Is she even aware of what happened up in the hills, of the vicious attack that put a man in hospital? Seconds tick by. She has to walk past the caravan to get to her car, and I can see her taking it all in, mentally documenting its details to share with her colleagues down at the station.

She checks the rear of the vehicle, but the registration plates have long since been removed. As she unlocks her car and moves to open the door, the faint flick of a heavy velvet curtain catches my eye, and the merest suggestion of a face, framed in the caravan window. My sharp intake of breath attracts her attention.

'I'm going to log the details of my visit, Ellie,' she says, regarding me closely. 'I'll call back in a couple of days, unless . . .'

I stand there, unable to move, unable to speak, conscious of the converging problems: PC Sampson, unwilling to leave; Shelby, hidden in the caravan; Dad, behind me, closing in. Words form themselves in my head and dissipate just as quickly. It's pointless. My body sags, too weary to fight. Lorraine will leave, and we will return to being Rooks, the family from the scrappie that the authorities can't touch.

As Lorraine gets into her car and starts the engine, Shelby's face swims into view again. His eyes are pleading, but I can't decipher the specifics. Help me? Run? Save yourself? My father's arm snakes around my shoulders as the squad car motors off.

'Look who we found in Aberdeen!' He raps his knuckles on the window and Shelby draws back. I surge forward to open the door, but the chain and the padlock are in place. Shelby is locked in, and I can guess who has the key.

'But he walked out of the hospital. He was staying with a mate.'

My father chuckles. The sound makes the hair rise on the back of my neck. 'Turns out we have the same mates! It's a small world, eh? Ah, here's the rest of the family!'

He opens his other arm expansively. Mum is there, clinging to River's arm. She wasn't expecting to see the caravan, and I can see the turmoil behind her expression. We all know that Dad always has an ace up his sleeve. And then she spots Shelby, or he spots her. It's a mutual thing. I can feel them drawing together. Shelby comes close to the window and Mum sleepwalks right up to him. She puts her fingers to the glass, and so does he. His are bandaged and broken.

'How touching,' Dad sneers. 'I knew how devastated you must be, my love, so I brought him home for you. Like a pilchard in a tin can!' He laughs at his joke. River stares at me, white-faced. What do we do now?

'If only we had a tin opener, eh, River?'

In the absence of Offshore Dave, River is the obvious stooge. I try to communicate wordlessly. *Don't play along*. His face is set, an expression I recognise. He's at war with himself. I clear my throat, finding my voice at last.

'Shelby's hurt. Let him out.'

'*Shelby's hurt*.' Dad repeats the words in a mocking sing-song. His arm drops from my shoulders as if I've contaminated him, and I can feel the sudden chill work its way into my bones. 'I have a better idea. How about we let your mother in?'

Mum makes a small noise, hardly an objection, but he moves over to her, takes her by the shoulders. 'Imelda, my love. All's fair in love and war, isn't that what they say? I'd never stand in the way of what you want. *Never*.'

I try to grab her attention, but her eyes are fixed on him, as if she can't look away.

'I think you two should be reunited,' he continues. 'A final ride in the old van.'

He swings around and punches the door of the caravan so hard it leaves a fist-shaped dent. I imagine Shelby wincing on the other side. I shouldn't be surprised by this zero-to-sixty surge into violence, this combination of slow, cold words and hot, sudden irrationality. I should be used to it, after all this time, but Dad always has the capacity to shock. Unpredictability is power.

'We'll get you on board, Imelda, and take a nice little jaunt into the country. Maybe back up the mountain. You like it up there, don't you? You and Shelby, the love of your life, all cosied up in the caravan. Very cosy.' He holds out his hand. 'River – the key.' My brother hesitates. *Don't do it. Don't give him the key*.

It's Mum that surprises us next.

'No,' she says, quite clearly. Her focus swings once more to Shelby. She looks at him through the caravan window. Holding his gaze. Holding the line. 'Leave him out of this. This is between you and me, Lawler.' She shakes herself a little, flexes her arms. 'I'm going to do what I should have done long ago. So many times, I've stood on the top of that waterfall and thought about it. Just one slip. Just one step, one foot after the other, and it would all be over . . .'

Something flickers on Dad's face. Fear, perhaps.

'If I take myself out of the equation,' she says, 'what then?'

She smiles – a whimsical kind of smile that chills me almost as much as Dad's physical violence. River and I speak at the same time: *No!*

But it's too late. She has a plan.

39

'What are you saying? Mum!' I launch myself at her, grasp her hand. I don't realise we're touching until she slips away from me. She strides off, coat flapping round her legs. And then she starts to run. Like Finella, she starts to run. There's a moment where we stand and watch her go.

'Run, Finella! Get out of there!'

'And Finella slips through a hidden tunnel and runs, and keeps on running, dodging the king's men-at-arms. She leads them a dance across the Howe of the Mearns, over the hill which now bears her name, Strath Finella, and here to this deep, dark gully. She's a woman of the woods – she knows when to hide and when to break cover . . .'

The old story comes back to me now – a fragile thread between us, stretched to breaking point. But it can't be allowed to snap.

'Mum, come back!'

I hear River's voice too, a deeper version of mine, but at first his words don't register.

'Run, Mum! Keep going! Don't come back!'

I swing round to him. 'What are you saying? She's going to drown herself!'

He points at my father, rooted to the spot, shell-shocked. 'Ask him what he's got in the fucking car boot. Ask him!'

When no one speaks, River gives the game away. 'Three containers of petrol. Dad has a plan too.'

I'm swallowed up by the yard, the wasteland, the woods. I dodge the roots, the scrap and the buried parts. I pass the birches and the pond and the car cemetery, but she is always ahead of me. I see her coat flapping through the tree trunks, the flash of her hair like a crow's wing, but she will not stop. At one point, I hear crashing behind me. I'm being followed, but none of that matters now.

Mum is dancing now, through the bracken and heather, and I'm skipping after her. I can hear hounds whining, men shouting. Mum stops for dramatic effect within sight of the waterfall. The tremendous thunder of it enters our hearts and snatches away our voices.

'They say she took to the trees, walking across the tops of them to escape.'

'Could she have? Was she magic?'

A wind has got up from somewhere. It takes my breath away. The topmost branches have a language of their own, a sort of keening, and it's easy to imagine Finella up there, perched on a limb, looking down. What would she think of us? You had no choice, Finella, but my mother does. I don't know why she would choose to leave us.

I push myself onwards, to the difficult paths that overlook the gorge. The water is crashing below, and, as always, that heady thrill makes my heart skip a beat. The air is different, moist and cold. One slip and it's all over.

I catch sight of her at last, on the crumbling viewing platform. Her coat is a brighter green than the living things, the grass and the leaves and the undergrowth. She's standing at the top of the falls, where everything collapses into nothingness. One slip. Oblivion. I creep closer.

'Who knows what you can do when you need to escape the inescapable?'

'Mum . . . Mum! Come back.'

The crash of the water whips away my words before they get to her. Mum takes a step closer to the edge of the falls. Stares straight ahead, hands on hips like a warrior queen. Beyond her, there is only a wet mist. When she glances back at me, her face is in shadow. There are dark mysteries in her eyes which I now understand. She stares out at the emptiness, a still, lonely figure on the edge.

'What are you thinking?' I shout. 'Are you crazy? You had a chance to tell the police. It was your chance to get away from him, get him locked up!'

She shakes her head, and I recognise that little gesture of futility, of powerlessness. I grew up with it. 'I can never be free of him. You think the authorities can keep me safe?' She gives a chilly little laugh. 'Look at what he did to Shelby, what he's planning to do to both of us.'

'But you can press charges! Lorraine says, what he's done to us, it's criminal. All you have to do is tell her your story and she'll do the rest. Why are you shielding him?'

'I can't go through that, testifying against him in a courtroom. Do you really want me to put your father in prison? What would that do to River? And anyway, don't tell me Offshore Dave wouldn't be waiting for me outside. There's no hiding place – your father will always be pulling the strings. I have to do what I should have done all along.'

Suddenly, River blunders out of the woods, breathing heavily.

'Dad's right behind me – he's spoiling for a fight. And that policewoman must have connected the caravan with reports of what happened in the hills. She called for backup. There's at least two cars just pulled into the yard.'

I try to shush him, but the water takes up the sound and hurls it into the abyss. Everything is careering down a sixty-foot drop: water, sound, reason. I wail my mother's name again, and she looks back for a second. Her eyes are dull with resignation.

'Don't do it,' says River. 'Not now. You're safe now. It's over.'

He tries to push past me, but I grab him, thinking he'll make it worse. And then Dad explodes on the scene. His blue eyes are wild and searching. He looks past us and sees Imelda, standing at the edge of the falls. I expect him to bellow at her, but instead, he tells us to stand aside, and he picks his way towards her over the mud.

'Imelda, darling. It's all right. You're safe now.' His voice is honey. 'Come back now. Come home with me and we'll get this sorted out.'

'You're not listening!' my mother yells. 'You've never listened to me!'

She's competing to be heard above the cacophony of the waterfall. It's ironic, somehow, that the one time she raises her voice to him, the effect is lost.

'It's dangerous up here, Imelda. I've always said it: these paths are treacherous. You're too close to the edge.'

'Mum, come back with us and let's talk,' I butt in. It's time she listened to me, not him. The two of us are doing a weird sideways creep towards her, like hounds about to fight over a rabbit.

He eyes me coldly. 'I've got this. Take your brother away.'

'No. I'm not leaving her with *you*.'

He narrows his eyes at me and opens his mouth to speak, but Mum interrupts. 'I'm too scared to move, Lawler,' she says. 'You'll have to come and get me.'

Something like fear passes across his face. This is not his place, the den. It's not part of his kingdom and he doesn't understand it. He doesn't know where to put his feet, or how to get a grip. He's at home with grease and grime, not earth and water. But he doesn't want to lose her.

'I'm coming, sweetheart. I'll take you home and you can tell me what's bothering you.'

Sweat breaks out on his brow as he inches closer. I'm close, too. Right behind him. I meant it. I won't leave my mother with him. Never again.

He reaches out a hand to her, but she doesn't take it. She's facing him now, smiling, although there's a strange light in her eyes. Maybe he sees himself reflected there, because there's a moment when he pauses. There's a space, a gap in time, when even the water goes quiet.

40

I'm back in the kitchen with a blanket round my shoulders. A paramedic is checking me over; I think I'm being treated for shock. There's a lot of police activity in the yard, and Julie, who's sitting next to me, is stroking my hand. I can't think why she's here. Maybe someone called her. She says there's a helicopter hovering over the Den of Finella. River is being questioned separately, in the sitting room. It's routine, according to PC Sampson, to separate witnesses, see if their stories stack up. When my brother was led away he was weeping and distraught, but he's a Rook. We know how to hold the line.

As well as Lorraine, there are two detectives in the kitchen. They're having a hushed conversation over by the cooker, after listening to my version of events.

'There's a gap in my memory,' I wept. I just can't remember exactly what happened. All I remember was that there were three of us standing at the top of the waterfall, and then there were two. Just like that. It's all very hazy, but it's treacherous up there, especially after that heavy rain. It only takes one slip.

The detectives were gentle and understanding; I expect Lorraine has discreetly aired our dirty laundry in the appropriate circles.

'You poor thing,' says Julie for the umpteenth time, rubbing the back of my hand. 'By some miracle, you get your mum back, and on the *same day* this happens. Oh my word. What are the chances?'

Lorraine swoops in on my other side. 'Things will proceed in the same way, Ellie. We've mounted a search, but as you know from last time . . . We'll be looking for proof of life, and the more time a casualty spends in the water with no sighting of them, the less chance there is of a positive outcome. However, police divers will be conducting a thorough search of the coast. You just never know.'

I catch a glimpse of something in Lorraine's eye. What is she thinking? That if I'm capable of misleading the police about my mother, what else am I capable of? Losing a second parent in a matter of weeks – unlucky or deliberate? I'm still trying to decipher her expression when the door opens.

My mother sidles in. They've allowed her a few minutes with Shelby, who is sitting in the ambulance. Julie says they got him out of the caravan with bolt cutters because no one knows who has the keys. I think he's going to be taken to the hospital, despite Mum's protests. 'He's family,' she'd said. 'I need him here.'

Only I notice the first flush of hope beneath her skin. I have a sudden urge to contact Piotr, to explore an unspoken possibility. Lots of things seem possible now . . .

At the end, she had no choice.

'Do you think she survived?'

Mum stoops to brush the hair away from my face. 'What do you think?'

Acknowledgements

As ever, I'd like to take this opportunity to thank the many people who helped bring *Ellie Rook* to life. My wonderful agent, Jenny Brown, and the lovely team at Polygon – Alison Rae, copy-editor Julie Fergusson, Jan Rutherford, Kristian Kerr, Lucy Mertekis, Jamie Harris and anyone I've missed – plus the amazing Fiona Brownlee.

Thanks to my amazing friends, neighbours and family who always give me such encouragement, and the readers, reviewers and book bloggers who have been so generous in their support of my efforts. And I'm deeply grateful for the valuable insight and information I received from professionals working in domestic abuse services.

The legend of Finella is a fascinating one; thanks to Kerry Fleming and renowned artist and printmaker Sheila Macfarlane, who brought her to my attention. I'll never forget the day Sheila invited me to her studio and unrolled her magical scrolls of Finella leaping the falls! Check out her powerful woodcuts here: www.sheilamacfarlane.net/the-finella-prints.

Although I've taken a few liberties with geography in this novel, Scotland's east coast landscape is dotted with evidence of Finella's existence: place names, ruined towers and tree-studded mounds. Records show that she was a noblewoman, a huntress, a strong and daring woman who killed a Scottish king in revenge for the murder of her son. Pursued by the king's men, Finella fled through the glens and evaded capture until she was stopped by the waterfall. Her only option was to jump. I wanted to say something about the lives of women who feel they have no choice.